REVELATION

Other Books in This Series from Peter and Paul Lalonde

Apocalypse (Book #1)

Tribulation (Book #3)

Judgment (Book #4)

REVELATION

PETER AND PAUL LALONDE

THOMAS NELSON PUBLISHERS®
Nashville

Published in Nashville, Tennessee, by Thomas Nelson, Inc.

Scripture quotations are from the following sources:

The KING JAMES VERSION of the Bible.

The REVISED STANDARD VERSION of the Bible. Copyright © 1946, 1952, 1971, 1973, by the Division of Christian Education of the National Council of the Churches of Christ in the U.S.A. Used by permission.

Library of Congress-in-Publication Data

Lalonde, Peter.
     Revelation / Peter and Paul Lalonde.
          p. cm.
     ISBN 0-7852-6692-5
     1. Rapture (Christian eschatology)—Fiction. 2. End of the
world—Fiction. I. Lalonde, Paul, 1961– II. Title.
     PS.3562.A4147 R48 2001
     813'.54—dc21   2001031499
                                                                    CIP

Printed in the United States of America
01 02 03 04 05 PHX 5 4 3 2 1

To the Cloud Ten Team.
We could not be more proud of you,
or more honored to be counted
among your friends!

Chapter 1

THE MAN POSITIONED HIMSELF behind a grove of trees in a small lot at the end of a suburban cul-de-sac. It was the school bus's last stop for the three children living in the houses along the block. The children each had a neck chain from which hung a house key. It would be another hour before any adults returned to the neighborhood, and by then he would be gone.

He had a high-powered air rifle with telescopic sight, designed for shooting small game in silence, though the one he carried had been modified for greater velocity and penetration. It could kill a man at twenty-five feet, something he had proven himself more than once. Today no one needed to die. He only needed to cripple the school bus long enough to examine the undercarriage in order to know exactly where to attach an explosive device.

Bracing against a tree, carefully aiming the rifle, he waited until the last of the children had stepped out and the bus was pulling away. The dart went directly into the side of the right rear tire, penetrating deeply, creating a slow leak, allowing the bus to go a mile or so before the driver would stop to check. Then he would arrive, posing as a good Samaritan.

He covered the rifle with leaves and dirt and cut through the woods to where his car was parked. He already knew the bus's route and knew that if he hurried, he could intercept it before the driver limped to the garage or called for a tow.

It took ten minutes for the man to reach the bus. The driver had pulled it to the side of the road where he turned on his flashers and looked for the damage.

"Got a problem?" the man asked, getting out of his car.

"I kept asking them at the garage to check the tires," said the driver. "Check the tires. They buy us seconds to keep school costs down. Never think about what could happen with a busload of kids."

The man dropped to the ground, lay on his back, and put his hand underneath, feeling the surface. The blast would tear into the undercarriage, lifting the bus, sending shards of metal through the interior. Proper placement would mean none of the children inside could escape without being wounded. The news media would have a lead story of carnage for the top of the hour.

Having satisfied himself he could do the job he had been ordered to do, he sat back up and said, "Lucky you weren't going very fast or you'd have broken an axle getting it stopped. You call for a tow yet?"

"Yeah," the driver replied. "Guy came by with a car phone. Let me call the garage."

"There's nothing more I can do," said the man. "If you're okay, I'll be on my way."

"Thanks for stopping," said the driver. "Most people wouldn't get themselves dirty just to help a stranger."

"Hey, we're all in this together, you know what I mean?" the man replied, getting back into his car, then driving away.

∞

Thorold Stone tried to pretend he was lost in thought over the latest memo from Overlord Parker. But he wasn't fooling anyone as he passed through the O.N.E. agents' locker room. Still, if he was lucky, he could get by without being noticed.

"Hey, Stone," a voice called, "heard about your big bust today."

It was Lloyd Jemison, the biggest mouth in the department. Stone ignored him.

"Overlord Parker should give you guys a medal for taking out all those Haters," Jemison continued.

"We made the world a better place for the Messiah," murmured David Smith, Thorold's partner.

"How big a bust was it?" Jemison persisted. "Ten Haters? Twelve?"

"It was twelve and Crazy Annie," called Sam Goldfarb from across the room. "Lady Jesus and her disciples. I was there when they brought them in. Smelled like they hadn't bathed in weeks. How long did it take you to fumigate the van, guys?"

"They were creating a public nuisance," mumbled Thorold. "Uniformed should have handled it like they've always done when she stops taking her medication. We only got the call because she had a Bible this time. That made it a felony." He frowned. "I'll tell dispatch to give it to you guys the next time the old lady leaves her pills at home."

"Touchy, touchy," scolded Jemison. "You know what Overlord Parker says about our jobs. We're representatives of the big man himself when we help the people cleanse the streets for the Day of Wonders. We each have to pull our weight."

"She had a Bible, remember?" said Smith angrily. "Probably never opened the book, but Parker's going to want us to go door-to-door to see who was keeping illegal books instead of turning them in."

"They'll get a medal for sure." Jemison laughed. "Maybe they'll even be allowed to use Overlord Parker's parking space for a week."

Thorold felt like punching someone. He knew Overlord Parker would have Crazy Annie locked up someplace and forced to take her medication until she was stable again. The twelve drunks would be tossed in the holding tank until they dried out, not one of them a Hater. As for the Bible, when Annie was back on her pills, she probably wouldn't be able to remember what Dumpster she found it in. And for all that, he and Dave would have to write up thirteen separate arrest reports and spend at least a day in court telling the same story over and over again.

Stone and Smith hurriedly walked to the police parking lot. It was late, after 10:00 P.M., and they wanted to get home. Smith had a wife who was waiting. Stone had a six-pack of beer, his VCR, and too many memories. They didn't pay attention to the two men in suits who were driv-

ing into the back entrance of the One Nation Earth headquarters, an area used only for maintenance. The only person who was authorized to be back there was the supervisor
of the large laundry room that handled the cleaning of uniforms. Maybe whoever was driving the car was just picking
her up at the end of the workday.

∽

"Did you see who it was?" asked one of the two men in the
dark sedan as they pulled into the O.N.E. maintenance
area, their headlights off and the dome light unscrewed so
they could open the door without being seen.

"Looked like Thorold Stone," answered the other. "I'm
surprised he didn't swing back to take a closer look. Since
he lost his family, he's tried to be Super Cop. Works long
hours. Never off duty. Sticks his nose into everything to
keep his mind off what happened to his wife and kids."

The first man smirked. "That type usually ends up eating
his gun."

The second turned to look behind them. "We'd have to
delay our mission if he came to investigate. Let's be thankful he's having an off day."

The other nodded. "That was a lot closer than I like,"
he said.

The men left their car, one carrying an attaché case,
the other with a miniature camera in a small leather case on
his belt. To it, he attached a tiny but powerful flash attach-
ment and advanced the film in readiness.

The one with the attaché case stood by the employee

exit near the laundry, while the man with the camera positioned himself to grab the next person coming out.

It was the laundry woman who came to the door where a blinding flash exploded in her face. She felt hands grabbing at her, one covering her mouth so tightly her teeth cut into her lip, the other wrapped around her waist, pushing her back inside the laundry area, her arms wrenched behind her back, her wrists tied with a rope. A thick cloth was pulled between her teeth and another was secured over her eyes. Unable to speak or see, she was carried back into the laundry room and tied to a chair.

"We won't be long," said one of the men as he walked over to the rack of maintenance uniforms ready for the morning shift. He selected an O.N.E. Bus Maintenance uniform, then found another one, a size larger, for his partner.

While the second man dressed, the first, already in the uniform, opened the attaché case and checked the contents. There were two pairs of gloves, a small bomb, a detonating device, receiver, magnets, and duct tape for attaching the unit, a penlight, two remote controls, and spare batteries. "Everything's ready," he said, reaching in to remove a Bible with several pages tabbed by Post-it Notes, and a handful of religious tracts. "I'll leave the reading material with our tied-up friend."

"Don't struggle," said the second man to the woman. "The surveillance cameras will see you when we leave. Somebody will come by for you. In the meantime, relax. You're not going anywhere."

The men gathered their clothing and started to leave. As they reached for the door, the second man turned back and said, "And remember, a little less starch, please!"

∾

The restaurant was dimly lit with soft jazz enveloping its customers like a warm blanket. It was a place to begin a romance, celebrate an anniversary, or mend a broken heart. The food was like the ambience, prepared with subtle lingering flavors, while the service, though attentive and responsive, never intruded on the privacy needs of the diners.

Overlord Len Parker sat in a booth in the rear, a beautiful blonde as his dining companion. She was wearing an expensive designed dress, her hair wrapped in a chignon, a diamond pendant on a gold chain around her neck. She had the elegance of a woman born into money, at home with luxury and wealth.

"You realize I could have you killed if you don't please me," Parker was saying, holding the woman's hand and looking deeply into blue eyes that seemed to dance with the flickering of the candles.

"Yes, Len, I do," she replied softly, smiling tenderly at him.

"I could have you killed and no one, not even your father, would dare to question what happened to you," Parker continued.

"That's what I find so exciting about you," she replied. "My father speaks and ten thousand employees in five countries of the world jump at his word. You speak and whole nations tremble." She shivered involuntarily. Like a lamb frolicking near a lion's den, she knew at any moment she might be devoured, and the excitement and danger were like a powerful, addictive drug.

"Do I please you, Overlord Parker?" she asked teasingly.

"For the moment." He laughed, delighted with this woman who was as brazen as himself. He dated very little anymore, saw little reason for it. But that night, with the preparations for the Day of Wonders almost complete, he needed to relax with someone whose values and morality closely matched his own. "You're really very beautiful."

"And you are . . ." She paused for a moment, trying to find the right word. He wasn't handsome exactly, not like a movie star. Yet he radiated something, a subtle aura of violence that she found immensely exciting. ". . . you are the man I've dreamed about all my life."

"You must have very interesting dreams," he commented.

"All the other men I know are like Daddy," she continued. "They have money, but so do I. They have influence, but so do I. What they don't have is . . . forgive me for saying this . . . ruthless, cold-blooded instincts. That's a trait that can change the world if you know how to use it."

"It's the nature of my job, I'm afraid," said Parker.

"It's the nature of the man," she countered. "The job exists because of who you are, not the other way around." She leaned forward. "Have you ever personally killed a Hater?" she asked. "Was it self-defense?" she probed. "Did you have to kill them?"

"Sometimes it was self-defense. Most times it wasn't. Does that trouble you?"

"No. I find it delicious. If you and I decide to keep seeing each other, can we still be together after the Messiah reveals his plan?"

"I have no idea," he answered. "Let's just enjoy the moment."

"After dinner, will you take me back to your office building and show me where you keep the Haters?" she asked.

"It's not a pretty sight," he replied.

She smiled. "That's what excites me. Whatever is done to those despicable people is never enough. Isn't this a wonderful time in which we're living?" she added happily as the server brought their food.

Chapter

THE STORAGE AREA WAS LOW SECURITY. There were no cameras, no alarms. Just a high chain-link fence open at the driveway, the entrance chained and padlocked at night so the buses could not be driven off the grounds. No one thought about someone coming in to attach a bomb. No one thought someone would ever endanger the lives of children.

The uniforms the men had stolen were a precaution. O.N.E. personnel would have no interest in anything taking place around the garage, but the security service that covered the maintenance yards might have someone patrolling nearby. More likely the person was making rounds and thinking about where to take a nap. Nothing ever happened in most of the maintenance yards except an occasional vandal with a can of spray paint.

The men in the stolen maintenance uniforms worked quickly and quietly to attach the bomb near the rear axle of the bus. "Got to make certain it's high enough to clear the ground," said one. He slid underneath the bus while his partner stooped down holding the flashlight. Using a powerful magnet he secured the explosive detonator and radio receiver. "Otherwise they're liable to roll over a rock or curb and knock it off."

"You're sure it can't go off accidentally?" his partner asked nervously.

"I'm using a variation of plastique," replied the other. "You could roll it into a ball and play catch with it. That's why it's always been popular with terrorists."

"You sure you've got enough?" asked the other.

His partner smirked. "You wouldn't want to be sitting within ten feet of this when it goes off."

❧

The maître d' was apologetic as he approached the table where Len Parker was dining. "Mr. Parker, we have a telephone message for you," he said and handed Parker a slip of paper.

He glanced at the message, then turned to his beautiful companion, "Would you mind if I made this call? I'm afraid it might be important."

"Far be it from me to interfere with the man helping to determine the fate of the world," she replied.

"Parker, here," he said into the phone and listened for a moment.

"It is curious that they'd go to all that trouble to steal two bus maintenance uniforms," he said at last. "But you're right. The Bible they left with the woman must mean they're Haters. Get the day shift commander to check for vandalism." He hung up.

"Something serious?" asked the woman.

"Just odd," he replied. "At least two men broke into the O.N.E. laundry area and stole two maintenance worker uniforms."

She raised her eyebrows. "And for that they had to interrupt your dinner?"

"Whoever did it left a Bible with marked pages," he explained. "That makes it a Hater crime and I have to be alerted the moment such problems are discovered."

She shook her head. "Haters. That's all you hear about anymore. Why anyone would want to be a Hater is beyond me. They're such righteous fools. I just wish they'd shut up and go away."

"We're trying to handle them," Parker reassured her. "That's why we have the reeducation camps to help the ones who can be saved for the Messiah."

She wet her lips and smiled. "Remember, you promised to take me to see where they're kept after dinner."

ᘓ

They moved as they had been trained, converging on the neighborhood from several different streets. The minivan that served as the mobile command post looked like any other family vehicle, the sophisticated communication equipment hidden by tinted windows, and the specialized antennas built into the roof that made them impossible for a casual observer to spot. The high-tech weapons were concealed in a picnic cooler and in shopping bags from the neighborhood supermarket. There was nothing to identify them as a unit of the One Nation Earth Division Four Tactical Strike Force.

The operatives of Division Four had been specially selected for both their skills and their ability to blend in to the neighborhoods where they operated. The Tactical Unit was a diverse team with two members in their fifties, two in their thirties, blacks, whites, a Hispanic woman and an Asian: the type of people common to a neighborhood coffee shop, each so carefully briefed that their actions seemed completely normal.

The oldest couple was a man wearing a rumpled suit and carrying a battered briefcase, and a white-haired woman wearing a simple housedress. They walked up the driveway first and, if the tenant, one Jack Braxton according to the computer printout, spotted them, he would see only salespeople or perhaps someone looking for an address. But Braxton didn't spot them. And the man dropped to one knee, opened his case and, taking out what looked like a flare gun, loaded a shell and fired into the house. The window exploded, shards of glass covering the living room and sending a sleeping German shepherd yelping into the kitchen, his legs and head bleeding from several cuts. Braxton emerged from the kitchen just as a second shell struck the floor, exploding with a deafening roar. It was a concussion grenade, and the sound was meant to stun and disable anyone within range.

It was a signal for the others to make their move. In orange-and-black O.N.E. caps for easy identification, they raced up the driveway, taking positions in front and back, then kicked in the doors, grabbed the man, and threw him to the ground. He was made to lie face down, his hands out to his sides, his legs crossed at the ankles. As one officer kept his knee in the small of the man's back, a high-voltage stun gun was pressed against his shoulder.

The strike force team moved from room to room, weapons drawn, checking for other residents. The dog had recovered enough to come looking for his master, baring his teeth, growling, and slowly advancing on the strangers.

In a corner of the room, Agent Jane Kilman was opening drawers to a desk, which held a computer, a small stereo unit, and a book-filled hutch. When she heard the dog, she turned, aiming her handgun at the animal, and fired a single round to its head. The dog dropped instantly and the man on the floor screamed, starting to rise. The officer holding him down squeezed the trigger of his stun gun and the man convulsed wildly, his body shaking, his pants suddenly wet as he lost control.

Finding the house empty, the team began a methodical search, emptying desk drawers and removing them to see if anything was hidden behind. The lid of the toilet tank was removed, heater vents were opened, and bed mattresses were pulled off and ripped apart. Eventually, the team found the contraband they had been seeking, the material Jack Braxton had advertised on the Internet, thinking he was safe from detection. But he didn't know about the sting operation or the "lock back" program O.N.E. internal security technicians had installed to instantly trace the source of anyone making contact with the Web site created as a false front for "Operation Mop-up."

"We found all five," said one agent. "Three King James

and a couple of New International Versions. He must not have found any takers for this Hater trash."

"And whatever was on the computer is gone now," said his partner, laughing. While the others had searched, she had run an electromagnet across every inch of the equipment, erasing all files on the hard drive.

The five books were placed on the floor of the living room, doused with gasoline, and set on fire. As the team prepared to leave, the agent who had been guarding the man still convulsing on the floor asked, "What about this Braxton? Should we take him in?"

"Leave him," said the unit commander. "If he recovers before the smoke gets him, he can spread the warning to other Haters."

"And if he doesn't . . . ?" asked the one who had shot the dog.

"One less Hater," sneered the unit commander. "One less threat to the Messiah."

ஃ

They had covered the story as if it were a routine assignment, the camcorder operator, sound tech, and reporter shooting the video and rushing it to the studio for a satellite uplink. It was scheduled for airing at six, then updated again for eleven.

Except this story was anything but routine. They knew that today there would be no six o'clock news. For them, there would be no six o'clock anything. Instead they would be witnesses to a world gone mad as they took their places on the streets of New York, Los Angeles, Chicago, Toronto, London, Rome, Paris, Tokyo, Moscow, Baghdad, and Tel Aviv to give viewers live coverage of their own deaths.

Long- and intermediate- range ballistic missiles armed with thermonuclear warheads were minutes away from vaporizing the most populated cities on the planet. Other missiles, armed with deadly nerve gas and biological agents such as anthrax, were targeted to eliminate the populations of the Middle East, Africa, and much of Asia. Resistance was futile, yet thousands of heavily armed soldiers were already moving through the valley of Megiddo. Fighter planes swarmed high above the ancient site while battle-ships and aircraft carriers, flying the flags of a dozen nations, were poised off the coasts of Europe, Africa, Asia, Australia, and North and South America . . . a show of force unlike any that had ever before been assembled. Yet when the lethal weapons had been launched, such armies and navies were like plastic toys in a child's game of soldiers.

The reporters who had taken to the streets knew all this and more. They knew that on a day when death was near, and the future was a nightmare beyond comprehension, they would be the only witnesses. Their cameras would record the anguish of parents whose children had perished; the last stolen kisses of lovers who would never meet again; the faces of the silent ones who had found reality too horri-ble and retreated into madness.

It was these moments, captured on tape three months earlier, that had been edited for Franco Macalousso's pleasure as he watched them in his private screening room in WNN's corporate headquarters. He relished the street interviews with close-ups of the faces staring at the sky, desperate for escape, knowing there was none. He delighted in the larger-than-life image of himself emerging from a helicopter on the Mount of Olives near the Western Wall in the city of Jerusalem, and still remembered the heat of that day, the dry earth whipped by helicopter blades, blowing in his face like tiny darts until he moved clear of the rotor.

The edited footage showed the missiles bearing down and faces of fear so intense it radiated into the viewing room. Macalousso momentarily froze the image of a toothless old man, tears filling his yellow eyes, his mouth open as if to speak, but nothing emerging from his parched throat. His dread was almost contagious and as his image filled the screen, Franco Macalousso smiled.

It was such fear he had come to treasure when he relived that awesome day, heart-stopping fear so terrible even the strongest men trembled. Give them fear and a sense of hopelessness, then take it away and they will give you undying loyalty. That was what he had proven to the world.

Macalousso released the "pause" button, watching the image of himself looking up at the sky, at the rapidly approaching missiles. He saw himself once again raise his hands above his head and shout, "ENOUGH! WE WILL HAVE PEACE!"

And then, in a moment no greater than the blinking of an eye, there was silence. Air traffic controllers were shown

staring at screens where the rapidly moving blips of unstop-
pable missiles had vanished. The amazed voices of pilots
could be heard reporting that the bombs they carried had
vanished from their bays. Soldiers were seen staring in
shock as their weapons vaporized around them. Political
leaders dropped to their knees, weeping like babies.

He stopped the tape then, knowing well how the story
ended. Smiling, refreshed, Macalousso stood and left the
room.

Chapter 3

THEY HAD COME TOGETHER hesitantly at first, Aunt Naomi and Uncle Ralph being the first to arrive at Jimmy's house. He hadn't seen them for six months or more, not since they had gone to a county fair and had so much fun.

The next time they came together, so much had changed. Grandma had disappeared. That was what they were telling the kids, the word his schoolteacher used when classes began after the "Day of Miracles." Everyone seemed sad and Aunt Naomi's eyes were puffy and red, so he knew she had been crying.

Aunt Peggy was the next to arrive that day, along with his cousin, Jessica. He rarely saw Aunt Peggy, and had only vague memories of Jessica, who was now eighteen. Even Uncle David, who usually got down on the floor to wrestle with him, seemed sad. "Not today, Jimmy," he said. "We grown-ups need to talk."

And talk they did. They were still going strong when Jimmy went to bed. He knew something was happening, but could not tell what or understand why everyone was so serious.

A "miracle" was what his mother had called it after everyone left. "We never got together like this before . . . before Grandma . . . disappeared. There were always too many quarrels."

It was still hard for his mother to discuss the day Grandma disappeared. One minute the older woman had been scolding her daughter for refusing to take him to church on Sunday and the next, she was gone, her clothing left in a neat pile on the floor.

"We thought she was wrong to push her beliefs on us," his mother had tried to explain. "The Bible was for a different time, for different people, but Grandma couldn't see that. She just kept talking about Jesus as a living presence like the Haters do. I just thank the Messiah for showing us that we have progressed beyond that. We all miss Grandma, Jimmy, and I'm sure Franco Macalousso would want us to remember her with kindness and compassion, but she was influenced by the Haters. So it's no wonder the Messiah removed her from our lives."

She grew silent then, filled with memories of her last encounter with the old woman. "You lived in a simpler time, Mom," Jimmy's mother had said. "There are different demands. We all have fond memories of those days, but the world has moved on beyond that outdated book you keep quoting."

Then, trying to appease her mother, she added, "I know you'd like us to go to church more often than we do. But it's just not what my generation is all about."

It was an argument they had all had with her, one they

expected would continue for years. Then, suddenly, their mother was gone. Ruth Davis Malone, seventy-two years old, by all accounts a gentle, loving woman, hardworking, caring, a good neighbor, and a good friend. Yet she was also rigid and unyielding when it came to "the word of God," and she had disappeared along with so many others on that awful, yet ultimately glorious day. She had left behind so many unanswered questions.

And now her children had come together as they had never done in her life, free from all the petty jealousies that had torn them apart. Free to enjoy a new heaven on earth, thanks to Franco Macalousso, the Messiah. Yes, many had vanished, but many more had been saved, and the sons and daughters of Ruth Davis Malone had found a common bond. The family was reunited. Love was reborn. Life began anew for them all, or so it seemed.

None of them could remember who made the suggestion that they meet regularly. But they began coming together every Friday night after work, alternating among homes, and sharing in the glory of the Messiah.

"Why is tonight different from all other nights?" Uncle David would ask as they stood around the dining room table where a picture of the Messiah, his arms upraised on the Mount of Olives, had been set. It was the same photograph that now hung on the walls of many homes around the world. But more important than the picture and the rituals was what his mother called "our own Macalousso miracle," the way they all felt deep inside, not condemning the choices each had made as adults, but respecting and accepting one another.

"Why is tonight different from all other nights?" Jimmy would echo. "Tonight we remember the coming of Franco Macalousso."

"Praise his holy name," responded his extended family.

"Tonight we remember his arrival on the Mount of Olives," Jimmy continued. "Tonight we remember the soldiers massed for war on the plains of Megiddo, the missiles just moments from their targets, the world on the edge of . . ." Jimmy always stumbled over the next word, even though Uncle David had written out what he called the family liturgy.

"Oblivion," whispered his dad.

"Oblivion," Jimmy repeated loudly.

"And who do we remember with sadness?" asked Uncle David.

"Grandma," said Jimmy. "And all the others who disappeared."

"Oh, Messiah, change their immortal souls," the others chanted. "Let them know the truth about your coming. Help them realize how they have gone astray, and reunite them with us in the New World Order, in the era of peace and love."

"We ask this of you, Franco Macalousso, the one who was promised," was Jimmy's next line.

"In your holy name," chanted the others solemnly.

✧

They moved down the streets as if they still belonged: a young woman on Rollerblades, enjoying a casual morning of exercise in Franco Macalousso Park; a young man dressed for tennis; an elderly man in tattered clothes shuffling along; a janitor in uniform on his way to work; a nightclub waitress in a low-cut blouse and thigh-high boots, moving to a beat only she could hear, each seemingly unconnected, each moving without urgency to no appointed gathering place.

A passerby might have heard a few words spoken barely above a whisper by these random citizens: "St. Mark's Cathedral." "First Baptist Church." "Community Church of God in Christ," and a closer observer would have seen them shudder for a moment, a tear coming to their eyes. Another church was to be destroyed, one more house of God was to be but a memory.

They would try to remind themselves that a church was only a building, a place for the gathering of the faithful, holy because of the worshiping community. The real church was ultimately in the hearts and minds of the believers, not in bricks and mortar that could be destroyed. But now, too late for the Rapture, they had come to better understand, to understand that their own bodies were the true temple of God. More important, they understood that wherever two or three gathered in His name, there He was in the midst of them.

They gathered furtively to hear the Word in basements, picnic pavilions at highway rest stops, and wherever else they would not attract attention. Churches were a glorious part of the past, but for today their lot was to be called "Haters," the despised ones, psychological lepers of a world gone mad.

So they moved about the city, trying to blend in, to look indifferent to what was happening, to seem like those who had proclaimed the new Messiah. They knew they could never speak the truth as they came to know it, that the so-called savior was not a deliverer but a deceiver.

☙

Carlton Filmore was late, and he hoped no one would notice as he hurried up the street to the rally. The gathering was larger than usual this week and he had to park more than a block from the old church, boarded up and covered with graffiti and posters declaring the forthcoming Day of Wonders. Nervously, he quickened his pace, anxious to get past this artifact from the dark ages, ashamed that he even remembered the name of the one called He Who Came Before.

Then he heard the music, voices lifted in song:

> Amazing Grace, how sweet the sound
> That saved a wretch like me.
> I once was lost, but now I'm found.
> The Messiah's come for me.

It was a variation of a hymn he remembered from his troubled childhood, a song his mother had sung when he was a boy. It had sounded so beautiful coming from her lips, so joyous. But he knew now that the Jesus she sang of was a myth, just a story people told to comfort each other. Jesus wasn't his friend. Jesus was his enemy. But that was before the Messiah came. Now he was a member of Macalousso's holy gathering, where he heard the music of his childhood with the new words and new understanding.

> The power of mind has been released,
> But for now it's just begun.
> The real powers won't be ours,
> Until we're truly one.

The singers were standing in a parking lot next to the old church, and seeing them Carlton felt at ease. They were united in purpose, gathered in triumph, and about to destroy the former gathering place of the Haters.

Loudspeakers set up around the parking lot enabled everyone to hear the uniformed member of Macalousso's regional leadership circle. Such men and women had taken the roles once held by local mayors and city managers, but their work had a spiritual side that raised the interest of those close to the Messiah.

"Three months ago, millions of people vanished from the face of the earth," the leader was saying, his voice echoing across the parking lot. "They were removed because of their unbelief, because they only knew the ways of hatred and division."

Cheers rose from the crowd and Carlton, normally a quiet man, found himself excitedly joining the shouts of "Praise the Messiah. Praise Franco Macalousso's holy name!"

"On that glorious day," the leader continued, "when the

lord himself returned and removed the chaff from the wheat, some feared we were seeing the end of the world. But today, thanks to our Messiah, Franco Macalousso, we all know that what we were really seeing was the beginning."

Carlton found himself crying tears of joy. *Thank you, Franco, my savior,* he said in silent prayer. *Thank you.*

The spokesman held up a waiting finger. "But not until we rid the world of the rest of those whose unbelief still holds us back will we be able to fully embrace our future," he continued.

More cheers as the speaker signaled to two overall-clad men in hard hats waiting beside some construction equipment. One climbed into the cab of a bulldozer while the other clambered onto a crane, raising a giant wrecking ball to batter down the bell tower of the boarded-up cathedral.

Later, when relating the incident to a friend, Carlton could not remember when the stranger had appeared. There had been nothing to draw attention to him initially until he rushed up and stood in front of the wrecking ball.

"Stop!" he shouted. "Stop! Don't do this! You're making a mistake! You don't understand!"

There was murmuring from the crowd, and a young woman shouted, "Look out! He's got a Bible!"

"A Hater!" shouted others. "He's one of the Haters."

"Franco Macalousso is an impostor. It says so, here, in the Bible!" the stranger proclaimed, raising a copy of the forbidden book above his head, like a warrior brandishing a sword of righteousness.

For a moment the gathering hesitated, then, in clusters of two and three they moved forward, closing in on the Hater, their faces full of anger and disgust.

"I'm not a Hater," shouted the man, his face slick with sweat, "I come in love in the name of our Lord and Savior Jesus Chr—"

The first blow struck with such force it broke his jaw. The second struck him in the stomach, doubling him over. He fought to catch his breath, to stay conscious and keep proclaiming the truth.

Uniformed officers of the O.N.E. special forces rushed in.

"Get back," came a shout from the mob. "We are the chosen people. We don't need the blood of a Hater on our hands. Leave him for the courts."

But the anger of the gatherers only grew. They had been freed from the past; freed from the guilt created by the falsehoods of Jesus. This man was a demon in their midst, a demon they would only exorcise by the spilling of blood.

The leader signaled the shaken choir and they resumed singing the rest of the hymn.

> He stopped the bombs, he froze our guns.
> He united soul and mind.
> The chaff has vanished. The earth is clean.
> The wheat has been left behind.

Carlton spotted a van moving up slowly, an emergency vehicle from One Nation Earth local headquarters, recognizable by the pyramid-and-eye symbol, the logo of Franco Macalousso's elite forces. Men and women in O.N.E. uniforms jumped out, pushing the mob back and checking the fallen Hater, who now lay on the ground, blood gushing from his mouth and nose. It was obvious only a miracle would save him now, and the Messiah would not work his wonders on unrepentant Haters.

As the stranger was loaded into the van, the choir finished its song:

> For those who still are not on our side,
> You cannot hide or run.
> There'll be no time to change your mind,
> When the Day of Wonders comes.

As the last voice lapsed into silence, the wrecking ball smashed into the bell tower with explosive force. Bricks shattered and shingles flew in all directions as the giant church bell fell with the agonized sound of the dying past.

The people watched in awe, then began to cheer spontaneously on this, a glorious Sunday morning!

Chapter 4

THOROLD STONE SAT as he had almost every night since the disappearance of his wife, Wendy, and their daughters, Maggie and Molly. Too tired to stay awake, too lonely to go to sleep, he lay on the recliner chair, staring at the television. On the end table next to him was a half-empty can of beer he'd been drinking . . . when was it? Three days ago? Four? A week? Wendy would have been annoyed with him for leaving it there, but she would have been angrier with him for drinking again. But he had gotten through that crisis, the loss of Wendy, Maggie, and Molly, the people he loved the most and the people he hurt the most.

Ten years ago, Thorold Stone was new to the force, and his captain's family had been murdered. The killer had gotten out of jail on a technicality and swore vengeance against the captain. The captain had thought nothing about the threats, assuming the man would be locked away for the rest of his life. He hadn't counted on a parole board that looked at the man's behavior in jail instead of what had put him there.

The captain had been devastated by his loss. If truth be

told, Thorold felt the captain had had it easier than him. At least the man had closure. He had buried his wife and his children and knew where they were. He could visit their graves.

Wendy and the girls had just vanished and that was the problem. He knew what the Messiah said about those who had disappeared and he knew that such a great and powerful man must know the truth. But he also knew his beloved Wendy, the woman he had loved since junior high school, a good woman who cared deeply for others. If she had followed a false prophet, she did it with a heart too pure to condemn her.

And the girls . . . What had they ever done wrong?

He looked at the television where a videotape shot when Wendy was first pregnant was playing.

Once, they had wondered if it was a foolish expense. The hundreds of dollars they spent on the camera seemed a needless extravagance. But they told each other the tapes could be seen by their grandchildren. And bring a joy in their old age as part of the Stone family history.

"Smile, Wendy," Thorold heard himself say as the camera zoomed in for a close-up of his beautiful wife. The image shook as Thorold had set the video camera down and moved into the picture with her.

He watched himself kissing Wendy passionately and he rose from his chair and went over to a bookshelf along one wall where pictures of the kids, on swings and at a county fair, had been set. He stared at his Police Academy training manuals, Wendy's nursing books, and her Bible, dusty and unused since her disappearance, now forbidden as subversive literature.

For a moment he thought cynically that he should arrest himself. After all, how many people had he sent to jail for owning that book? How many times had he heard someone say that the Bible wasn't his or her own, it belonged to a spouse, a child, a parent, or a friend, a reminder of happy times. It eased the sadness, he was told.

But he told himself he was different, that he held on to Wendy's Bible for different reasons. Yet he was an officer of the law, sworn to follow the orders of the Messiah. There were those who would consider his sin of omission cause for arrest or worse, and he knew that one day he would have to do the right thing and burn the Bible. But not now, not while he was still hurting so badly and not while the book seemed his one link to Wendy.

Finally drifting off to sleep, he had the same dream that had been haunting him since their disappearance, a dream both joyful and terrifying. He saw the girls, sitting on the swing set in their backyard. "Faster, Daddy!" "Higher, Daddy!" They giggled as he pushed them from behind. He sat on the ground with Wendy, watching happily, when the dream suddenly changed to a heated argument with Wendy, her begging him to read the story of Jesus, to try to understand why it was so much a part of her life. He just had to look at the Bible with an open mind and an open heart.

He was still in a deep sleep, yet it seemed as if his body was trying to avoid what always came next. "Daddy, Daddy, push us right up to the sky!" the girls would shout.

And in the dream he turned in horror to see his daughters vanish in a blinding flash of light, the swings still in the air, but the seats empty. Terrified, he turned to Wendy, but she was gone, too.

Thorold jerked himself awake as he had so many nights before, his body covered with sweat, his heart pounding rapidly. He bolted from the chair, forcing himself fully awake, and clutched the table, fighting for breath. A cry like a wounded bird escaped from his lips. Why couldn't he rid himself of the nightmare? Why was he tortured night after night?

The telephone rang, chasing away the dream. In the background he could hear a television newscast reporting on a speech by Franco Macalousso outlining the upcoming and much-anticipated Day of Wonders. The story had been the focus of the media for the past several days, and Thorold used the remote to silence the set as he answered the telephone.

"It's David, Thor," said the voice in the receiver. "There's been another bombing. I'll pick you up in a few minutes."

Taking one last look at the photograph of his wife and daughters, he went to the bathroom to quickly shave before meeting his partner.

಄

The crowd gathered on the fringes of the schoolyard was somber, standing silently and trying not to interfere with the grieving parents whose anguished sobs rang in the morning air. The Messiah had come. The world was supposed to be at peace.

It was difficult to comprehend that such violence was still taking place. A school bus filled with happy children had suddenly exploded; the ground littered with book bags and lunches along with the dead, the dying, and the wounded, whom ambulances were rushing to area hospitals. Police had sealed off the area and overhead, several helicopters from various radio and television stations hovered over the scene.

Thorold Stone and his partner arrived as the last of the injured were being loaded onto gurneys. The bomb had been located under the bus, a detective told them, lifting it up and flipping it on its side. Bodies were piled on bodies with some on the bottom wedged so tightly suffocation occurred before rescuers could reach them. Others were more fortunate, protected from flying glass and twisted metal by the children who had landed on top of them. It was a matter of sheer chance as to who died and who lived.

Even as they listened to a quick briefing, Thorold noticed a little girl resting on a gurney, with an IV in her arm. She was covered with blood and soot and for an instant he imagined she could be Maggie or Molly. This was real, not a dream, he told himself as he walked over to the little girl while paramedics prepared to load her into the ambulance. Her parents were not around. Thorold stroked her forehead and told her everything would be okay.

The child looked up, and turning to Thorold asked, "Why do they hate us so much?"

"I don't know, honey," he answered. "But we'll find them

and put them in jail where they can't hurt anyone else. I promise you that."

He watched as the ambulance sped out of the parking lot. David walked over, put his hand on his partner's shoulder, and asked, "Someone you know?"

"She reminded me of . . . ," he began.

"Yeah. I know," interjected Smith. "You okay to do some work?"

"I have to. I promised her," said Thorold, forcing his attention back to the crime scene.

"The bomb squad thinks they have a handle on the device that was used," said Smith as the two men walked to the charred remains of the bus, where a man was carefully examining an electronic device in a sealed plastic evidence bag.

"Miniature high-frequency receiver," said the investigator. "It's what we suspected when witnesses told us the bus exploded just as the doors opened. It had to be either connected with the door mechanism or a remote. We ruled out the door because that might have gone off anywhere along the driver's route. This is a line-of-sight receiver."

"You mean someone stood in the parking lot and activated it?" asked Smith.

"Risky," was the answer. "They might have been on an upper floor of the school, in a car on the street, or somewhere just outside the campus. But out here, with the school, and homes, and the businesses, the signal can't go far. No more than a mile in any direction is my guess. If you find enough of the transmitter, we can track it."

The bomb squad investigator was interrupted by the arrival of another O.N.E. officer. "Which one of you is Agent Stone?" he asked.

"Right here," replied Thorold.

"We got the source of the frequency transmission from the satellite review," said the officer. It's a warehouse, sir, used for a food cooperative a mile down the road on Front Street."

"I know the place. Come on, David, let's check it out," said Thorold.

Chapter 5

IT JUST DOESN'T MAKE ANY SENSE," said David as he and his partner drove to the warehouse. "All of these bombs, all of these killings, and what have they accomplished? They are only proving what the Messiah says about the Haters. Now the whole world wants to see them die. And for what? To be martyrs for a fraud like Jesus Christ? You can show ten people the same event and you'll get ten different reactions," he continued. "We all saw the start of the war at Megiddo and we all saw the miracle that day, the changes the Messiah has brought about. How can anyone see all that and not believe? How can they still have hearts so hardened they'd kill children to get attention?"

"Maybe that's the problem. Maybe we've all seen too much," replied Thorold.

"What do you mean?"

"Think about what this world's been through in the last three months," Thorold responded. "One minute we're all about to die in a nuclear war and the next millions of people vanish into thin air. The planet's been turned upside down. We're so busy trying to comprehend how we got into this situation, we're not thinking clearly."

"What are you getting at, Thor?" David asked.

"I don't know." Thorold shrugged. "I guess it's just that things aren't always what they seem. After all the years on the job we know that life isn't always fair. Bad things happen to good people. I don't understand why. They just do. But Wendy couldn't accept that. There had to be a reason. She started talking about God's will and God's mysterious ways. She got the kids really involved with the church, and next thing I know, she's praying it won't rain when we have a family picnic. It was her way of coping, I guess."

"And you're saying that calling Franco Macalousso the Messiah is our way of coping with all that's happened?" asked David.

"Yes. No. I don't know," was his frustrated reply. "Look at the facts, David. This guy claims he's God Himself and says he's responsible for all the miracles that happened. We're so relieved we're still alive, we buy into it. You know what they say. A drowning man will grasp at the point of a sword if that's all that's offered to him."

"The point of a sword?" replied the incredulous David. "The world was going to destroy itself and this guy stopped it. And you call that the point of a sword? I've learned one thing. It's what people show me that counts, not what they say or what they believe. And when the Messiah stopped the missiles, stopped the war, and saved the world, he made me a believer," conceded David. "He hasn't established his own church. He hasn't asked for money. He did what he did to save us from our foolish self-destruction."

"He made you a believer in what?" Thorold pressed. "Macalousso vaporized my family."

"But they wouldn't open their minds, Thorold," David countered. "You know that. He's explained it already."

"What kind of savior vaporizes sweet and gentle people just because he disagrees with them?" Thorold asked bitterly.

"They were holding the rest of us back," David insisted. "Besides, we don't know where they've gone. Maybe they're not dead the way we think. Maybe they're being reeducated somewhere. Maybe that's what the Day of Wonders is about. Maybe they'll come back."

"And maybe we should be considering alternatives, David," Thorold said darkly.

"Such as?"

"I don't know," Thorold admitted. "Maybe he's just a really good magician, only on some sort of cosmic scale. Or maybe he's just a guy who saw what was happening and jumped in to take credit. For all we know Macalousso is an alien from another planet." He sighed. "Look, all I'm saying is that someone should be asking some questions. Why am I the only one?"

"Because you're a cynic." His partner laughed. "And this hell you're going through over Wendy and the kids isn't helping. I've known you forever and you're always questioning. Even at the training academy, you were forever challenging the instructors. But what Macalousso did in Israel was all the proof I needed."

"Maybe that's because I'm not looking for God," Thorold snapped. "I'm just looking for my family."

The friends were silent as they approached the warehouse. Whoever had blown up a school bus might have booby-trapped their hideout. The Haters might be armed, ready to die a martyr's death.

Most of their work was peaceful. Most Haters were surprisingly gentle people, unarmed and unresisting. But the ones who had turned to violence were unpredictable. They slowly circled the block, discretely as possible given the situation. Plainclothes officers were positioned at all the escape routes. Smith and Stone parked their car around a corner and out of sight of the empty building. There they were met by an officer who handled the large dogs trained for such assignments.

"Everyone's in place," she said.

"Then I guess it doesn't matter if the Haters see us," replied Smith as he and Thorold put on their O.N.E. jackets. Thorold also took a shotgun from the car, chambering a shell while Smith took out a small electronic device.

"What's that thing?" asked the K-9 officer.

"A new toy a few of us are trying out," Smith responded.

"So what does it do?" the officer asked.

"It's supposed to read human DNA through solid concrete," David replied. "A dog's nose can't warn us of danger until we're almost on top of it. Heat sensors are good, but they can mistake a large animal or even a space heater for a human being." He held up the device. "This will only register a living, breathing person, someone behind a closed door or down a dark corridor waiting to blow us away."

"If it works," said Thorold skeptically.

The three officers and the dog moved swiftly down an alley leading to a fire escape on the abandoned building. Smith slowly moved the electronic device from side to side as a series of diodes glowed with varying intensity. Suddenly the dog whimpered and tugged on his handler's leash as she gave him slack and he moved to the door, sniffing. Smith walked up and held up the meter. It showed nothing.

"No one in there, boy. Whoever it was must have left," he said.

"I guess they can improve on Mother Nature," admitted the K-9 cop.

Suddenly the detector lights grew bright and Smith stopped, holding the meter steady to stabilize the reading. He activated the radio clipped to his jacket. "This is Smith. Stone and I are at the South End. We've got eighteen of them inside."

"Roger," said the voice on the radio. "Will dispatch."

Within seconds the armored van rolled into position and an O.N.E. SWAT team jumped out, ready for action. The undercovers moved into position, sealing the exits.

"Our orders are to shoot the Haters on sight," Thorold explained to the SWAT unit leader. "Tell your men to kill anyone who resists."

"Why is this a terminal operation?" asked the officer. "Is there something we need to know?"

"They bombed a school bus," Thorold explained. "They're obviously armed and dangerous. There might be explosives hidden in the building. My partner and I will go in first."

"That's not the way we usually do things," the team leader protested.

"We're doing it my way, Lieutenant," Thorold said sternly. "I want your men to hold fire until we have a chance to check the immediate area. If there's a problem, I'll give the signal. Is that clear?"

"Yes, sir," said the SWAT officer.

"Then let's do it."

Chapter

INSIDE WHAT HAD ONCE BEEN a corporate boardroom, eighteen men and women, young and old, black, white, Hispanic, and Asian, were on their feet, swaying and waving their arms as they joyfully sang:

> He has made me glad.
> He has made me glad,
> I will rejoice for He has made me glad.
> I will say this is the day that the Lord has made.
> I will rejoice for He has made me glad.

A half dozen people held Bibles as they sang with their eyes closed. Others held their hands in the air in joyous supplication, as if they were attending an old-fashioned revival meeting.

Smith and Stone were able to force open the door before the singing stopped, moving quietly inside followed by the O.N.E. SWAT team.

For an uncomfortable moment Thorold felt as if the people were aware of his presence, but would make no attempt to resist arrest. These were killers and he had seen the proof of their carnage. But why were they praying to Jesus? He was reminded of his wife, who would never have hurt anyone, but then the aftermath of the bus bomb crowded his mind. His heart hardened to the memory of these songs from earlier, happier times.

Victor Davis, once a reluctant member of the Mt. Olive Baptist Church, led the celebration, recalling with irony how his raptured mother had wept bitterly over his uncaring attitude toward God and the church. Now here he was, before a gathering of believers who regularly risked their lives to sing the songs he had so often avoided on Sunday mornings.

"Are you glad?" asked the man secretly called Elder Davis.

"Yes!" shouted the others.

"Are you really glad?" His voice became more fervent.

"Yes!!!" they answered with joy.

"Why?" he asked, his voice rising dramatically. "Why are you glad?"

"JESUS!" they responded delightedly.

"What blasphemy," whispered the SWAT team leader as he positioned himself in the shadows.

"They talk about Jesus and they've just blown up a school bus," said David derisively.

"They're true believers," Thorold whispered. "They think that whatever they do in God's name is somehow justified."

"That's sick." The SWAT leader grimaced. "People like that don't belong in our New World."

"That's why we're going to shoot to kill," said Thorold. Yet, even as he said the words, he thought of Wendy. He knew she would be in this secret church, standing with them to die if necessary. But why?

Elder Davis continued preaching. "I'm telling you tonight that there are those who don't agree with us. And why? Why don't they believe? Because they're looking with their eyes and not with their hearts. Well, I'm here to tell you, my friends, that seeing is not believing. No, sir. In God's world you won't see it until you believe!"

The congregation was shouting "Amen" and "Praise the Lord."

"Remember that our Lord and Savior said that wherever two or three are gathered in His name, He is in the midst of them," Elder Davis told them. "These times are like those of the early Christians. Families were divided. Christians were no longer welcome in society. Families considered their converted children as dead. There were pain and loss and much loneliness. They truly knew what it was to pick up their cross and follow Jesus. And that is where we find ourselves, keeping the faith in a world of fraudulent evil."

The eighteen now gathered in the warehouse were the largest gathering of Christians the O.N.E. agents had yet uncovered. Usually it was only two or three who gathered quietly in homes and abandoned buildings. The Davis congregation came together to re-create worship they remembered from childhood or from those times family members had made them attend Sunday worship. Back then they had not appreciated the community of the faithful, but now belief in

Jesus was a felony punishable by death; now they were called Haters and the whole world was against them. All they could do was stand together, even knowing the terrible risk.

"We've all got to walk by faith and not by sight," Davis continued. "We are living in an age of deception, delusion, and trickery. Whatever this impostor offers the world, it will be every bit as tempting as the forbidden fruit was to Eve."

"Amen, brother! Praise the Lord."

"That's why we have to look at the world with our hearts. That's why we have to let the love of God lead us every step of the way. And that's why the Bible says that only as a child shall we pass through the gates of heaven. Do you know what that means?"

Thorold could tolerate no more, remembering the sight of innocent children crying, helpless, and in pain. How could these Haters dare talk of loving children, yet still kill and maim such innocents? The preacher's words made him sick and he stepped forward, raised his pump-action shotgun, riveted on the face of the preacher.

"Let me guess what that means," said Thorold loudly. "That we should kill innocent children? Is that why you bombed the school bus? So they could get to your heaven?"

Elder Davis and the congregation stared in shock and confusion. Smith, holding a handgun, stood at his partner's side, and the remaining O.N.E. agents were in position. The Haters were surrounded by heavily armed officers.

"You're all under arrest," Smith barked, alert and vigilant for trouble. After all, these people lurked in the dark, planting bombs and plotting destruction. "Kneel on the floor and put your hands on your heads!" he shouted. "Now!" and the congregation obeyed.

The assault team moved forward, pulling the Haters to their feet and pushing them against the wall where they were carefully searched, handcuffed, and taken from the building. Most were silent as the officers searched for hidden weapons.

"I don't understand," said the handcuffed Elder Davis. "We're just Christians holding a worship service. We're not armed. We don't hurt people. It's not a crime to worship the true God."

"A school bus was bombed not far from here," Thorold snapped. "Schoolchildren, like the ones your Jesus is supposed to love, were killed and wounded."

"The Lord Jesus bless their souls," whispered Elder Davis, genuinely shocked. "Who would do such a terrible thing?"

"Have you looked in a mirror lately?" replied David angrily.

"We don't blow up things," he said, his shock changing to defiance. "If you think we did this terrible thing, you must have reason. But we're Christians. You must have heard the Bible when you were young. You don't have to be a believer to know Christians don't do such things. We're being set up."

"Shut up!" David commanded angrily. "The signal for the bomb detonator was traced to this building. Who else hides out in here?"

A teenage girl stepped forward. "Leave my father alone!" she said defiantly. A SWAT officer grabbed her by the arm until Thorold signaled him to let her go. "My father's not causing you any trouble," she continued.

"The truth causes these men trouble," Davis told his daughter, "and the truth has been in very short supply since Macalousso arrived."

"What is the truth?" Thorold asked, moving close to the pastor, his voice harsh, his size menacing. "You must think the Messiah is the devil in disguise."

"You think the devil is someone in a red suit with horns and a pitchfork," rebuked Davis. "If Macalousso is so good, why is everyone afraid to open a Bible? Why are you people destroying churches? If the Word speaks the truth and Macalousso is the truth, then why is he afraid to let people read the Word? We're going to jail for loving the Lord and you call this man the Messiah?"

"The Bible has been nothing but trouble for the world since the day it was written," Thorold snapped. "My wife read the Bible every day."

Davis, beginning to understand, asked softly, "She was one of the disappeared?"

"And my children," Thorold said, suddenly unsure why he was having this conversation.

"They're in heaven, young man," said Davis. "I believe that with all my heart. I lost my mother and sister and there isn't a day goes by when I don't cry myself to sleep over the loss. But we'd have been with them if we had listened. We'd still be together if some of us hadn't been such stubborn, self-deluding fools. I'll tell you this, young man. My wife, my daughter, all of us you see here today, are guilty of the same thing as your wife. We believe what she believed. We think as she thought. Do you actually believe she'd be blowing up school buses if she were still here?"

Thorold was shaken by the question, realizing this kind of talk could end up with him being evaluated for job fitness. He was on the edge and knew he'd better back away.

"Save it, Pastor!" he spat, more harshly than he felt. "You can tell it to the judge."

But that was a lie and he knew it. He didn't know what would happen to these people, but he was sure they wouldn't be going into a court of law. Macalousso's word was law now, and Haters were condemned to a fate Thorold didn't want to think about.

"If you'd just open your mind a little," Davis said quietly. "You seem like a good man. You seem like someone who . . ."

"I said, save it!" he snarled.

Then, so softly only Thorold could hear, the elder asked, "Why didn't you shoot us? Isn't that what you were supposed to do with dangerous subversives?"

"You just didn't look all that dangerous to me," replied Thorold.

"Can you get something out of my pocket without the others seeing?" the pastor continued quietly.

Thorold stood looking at him, saying nothing. He was probably going to have him take his Bible and try to turn him into a Hater. They were all devious and he had let his guard down, confiding anything in such a person.

"It's not a Bible, if that's what you're thinking," Davis whispered. "It's just an old romance novel even your Messiah hasn't banned, but it's important that you read it." He paused, staring intently at Thorold. "Really read it."

Thorold looked around, then reached into the pastor's suit pocket and pulled out a small, dog-eared book.

"Take it home with you," Davis whispered. "Read it from cover to cover."

"I'm not interested in Hater propaganda. I don't need conversion," Thorold insisted.

"I understand," said Davis. "This isn't about converting you. Take it. Look at it. Do it for your wife." He leaned forward, whispering, "There is a CD hidden in the front cover. It will tell you all you need to know."

"Time to move them out," said the SWAT team leader as he took the handcuffed Mr. Davis by the arm. Unresisting, Davis let himself be led to the door, then stumbled, barely able to keep his balance with his arms behind him. No one noticed as he tripped a nearly invisible signal button on the doorjamb.

Chapter

THE MORE HELEN HANNAH READ the books and pamphlets her grandmother Edna Williams had left behind, the more she felt herself connected to the earliest Christians. She read John's story of the disciples hiding in a room, Paul's letters to the early churches, and the stories of the Roman persecution of Christians whose faith was tested by certain death. From these early gatherings had come forth prophets, preachers, teachers, and leaders. They were often unlikely vessels of God's purpose and indecisive men and women until the Lord's hand touched their hearts forever.

Not that Helen thought of herself as one of them. She hadn't stood up to Macalousso and his followers or spoken the word of God for all to hear. She had not been made to choose between renouncing her love for Jesus and facing certain death. Instead she was hiding in an old bomb shelter beneath the sprawling WNN world headquarters complex, a place where few people bothered to go anymore.

It was John Goss, a former cameraman for WNN, who suggested that Helen and the other Haters use the shelter as a hideout. She had been wary at first, but had no better alternative.

She couldn't return to her apartment or go to the building where her grandmother had lived. And though she had dyed her newly cut hair, and changed her clothing to disguise her appearance, she did not know how long the charade would last. She left the shelter only during shift changes when it was easy to blend in with the crowd . . . it was her only chance to stay free, working with others to build the safe houses for the Haters in abandoned buildings and secret rooms all over the city. John Goss had developed a system of wireless communication devices between hideouts, which were also linked by computers and fax machines, tapping into telephone lines that could never be directly traced. It was Helen who had gotten the computer alarm that warned her of the warehouse raid.

"They got the Davises and their congregation," Helen told Goss sadly.

"What about the CD?" he asked breathlessly, hurrying over to the screen.

"There's no way of knowing," Helen replied. "We have to assume they got that as well."

"That CD was our only chance of trying to crack the code for the O.N.E. Day of Wonders," said Goss glumly.

"If it's gone, there will be another opportunity, a different opportunity. You'll see," said Helen.

Across the room Cindy Bolton slammed shut the book she was reading. "Another opportunity?" she cried, her voice shrill. "Another opportunity?" She turned to Helen and John, cocking her head to hear better. Dark glasses and a thick Braille edition of the New Testament were evidence of her blindness, but she was alert and tuned to the crisis they faced. "I have been trapped in this dump for three months," she continued.

"You people can change your appearance, sneak outside, see daylight. I can't disguise my blindness. I can't throw away my cane and pretend to walk the streets like everyone else. It was exciting at first, like being an Old Testament prophet. But then the walls started closing in. I know every inch of these rooms. That CD represented freedom for me, a way to prove Macalousso was a fraud, to turn the people against him."

Helen crossed over to hold the blind girl's hand. "Cindy, I'm sorry this has been so much rougher on you, but the CD wasn't a ticket to freedom. It was just another possible weapon against Macalousso. Sometimes we forget how much harder this is for you. But there's not a soul out there who wouldn't happily blow us to pieces if they got the chance. They don't know that we're being set up or that Macalousso is having us tortured or killed. All they see are the miracles, the magic show he has so carefully orchestrated. The tragedy is that it's working so well."

Cindy looked in Helen's direction for a moment, then picked up her Bible, running her fingers over raised dots to read the comforting words. She was through talking.

Helen watched sadly, realizing how much she had taken for granted, then rose from her chair and walked over to a command center that housed several computers, fax machines, a television set, shortwave radio, and other equipment. The wall above the equipment was covered with maps, papers, scrawled notes, and short Bible verses meant to help them sustain their vigil, along with a number of charts detailing Bible prophecy.

Ron Wolfman, a former military intelligence specialist, was their technical wizard.

"How are we doing, Ronny?" asked Helen.

"I'm set to access the O.N.E. personnel file," he replied. "I should be able to get in tonight disguised as a security agent. I've inserted some data in their system to clear me right through. But without the CD I really don't know what I'm looking for."

"Anything, Ronny," Helen replied. "Anything that will give us a clue about the Day of Wonders, even if it's just the key personnel assigned to the project. We've got to antici-pate what Macalousso is planning for us Christians."

"Is it going to be that bad, Helen?" asked Ron. "Macalousso controls the entire planet. Every Christian is either in jail or in hiding. What more does he want? What more can he do to us?"

"A lot," responded Helen. "The worst is yet to come. 'If they persecuted Me,' Jesus said, 'they will persecute you.' In fact, John 16:2 says, 'The time will come that whosoever kills you will think that he is doing God a service.'"

"And they call us the 'Haters' . . . ," mused Ron.

"Yes," said Helen. "Good is bad and bad is good. But Jesus also said in John 15:18 that if the world hates us to remember that it hated Him first, and not to worry because He has chosen us out of this world." She turned. "Does that help you any, Cindy?"

But the blind girl did not respond. She had set aside her reading, put on earphones, and was listening to music on a cassette player.

Ron laughed, noticing Helen's frustration. "And I'm sure Cindy's heart is in the right place," he said. "Right now she's hurting. Let her have her little escape. You can talk to her again later."

Chapter

S O MUCH FOR THE BIG RESISTANCE, huh, David?"
Thorold joked as he and his partner watched the Haters
being carted away.

"You know you disobeyed orders, Thor," David warned.

"I know what headquarters said," Thorold replied.
"Haters who kill are Haters who die. No mercy. No trial.
But that's assuming they are armed and resisting. That's not
what happened. For all we know, they had nothing to do
with the bombing."

"Thor, get real," his partner scoffed. "Just because they
had Bibles instead of bombs doesn't make them any less dangerous. We both know that when a thorough search is made,
we're going to find the detonator and they'll be executed."

"Don't tell me the Messiah wants us to act on emotion
and not knowledge," Thorold replied. "We're supposed to
be a government of laws divinely led. Isn't that what has
been drilled into us these past few weeks? If these people
are guilty . . ."

"*If* they're guilty? Thor . . . ," David interrupted.

Thorold frowned. "I'm sorry, David. I looked into the
face of Davis and all I could see was my wife arguing with

me. She was wrong, I'll grant you that. She followed a false god. Macalousso's made that very clear and I accept it. But Wendy would never hurt anyone." Thorold looked past his partner as he tried to get his emotions under control. "I just find it hard to believe these people could be responsible for killing those kids."

"We both know that appearances can be deceiving," David reminded him. "When I was on the homicide detail I worked on the unsolved murders of some construction workers. The deaths were violent and these guys were big, powerful men, not easy to kill. It took us months to find the killer, a sweet little old lady in her seventies who lived in a building slated for demolition. That crew was scheduled to handle the demolition. To look at her, you'd never think she was capable, but she eventually confessed." He put his arm on his partner's shoulder. "I checked the electronic satellite surveillance information myself, Thor. The signal that detonated the bomb came from this building. And you saw the DNA scanner. There's no one else in there."

"It could have been hidden by someone who knew they were here," argued Thorold. "Someone who wanted us to think the Haters were responsible."

David shook his head. "No way. That bomb was perfectly timed to maximize the death toll. Whoever set it off was watching, their finger on the button."

"So they'd at least have binoculars and a radio control. I didn't see any of those things when we made the arrests," Thorold persisted.

"The guys from the bomb squad will be going through

the place a lot more thoroughly than we did," David replied. "They'll find whatever was used.

"Look, Thor, I grant you they seem like nice people, but they're still Haters." He looked at his partner, seeing the depth of pain he still felt from the loss of his family. More quietly he continued, "Thor, I know how rough this has been for you. I know what that guy said must be eating away at you. I know you're shaken because of our shoot-to-kill orders. Maybe you were right to take them in. But they could still kill for their sick beliefs. We both know how fanatical these Haters can be. At least try to . . ."

"To what?" Thor snapped. "Keep an open mind?"

David started to say something, then thought better of it. They began walking, studying the building as they went around the side to an area partially overgrown with bushes, where they found a door. It was small with rusty hinges, but a closer look revealed that flecks of oxidized metal had been chipped away, indicating that the door had been used recently.

Thorold tried to turn the handle but the door was locked. "Give me that people-detector thing," he said.

"You think someone's inside there?" David asked softly.

"This door has obviously been used," Thorold mused. "Maybe it's the Haters' entrance."

Thorold aimed the device at the door, pressing the button and moving it slowly over the door. "Nothing," he said, picking up the shotgun and preparing to enter.

David also drew his weapon, then stepped aside as Thorold used a Karate sidekick to batter the door.

"One more and we're in," he said, striking it again as the hinges gave way.

cłə

Deep inside the warehouse three men sat silently in a room specially lined with material to deflect detectors. Metal shelving held electronic equipment meant for broadcasting and tracking, and a large reel-to-reel tape recorder had been attached to a scanner for intercepting cell phones, CB radios, and other signals. There were several VCRs, recording television broadcasts and connected to satellite dish receivers and remote-controlled video cameras, as well as an observation window made invisible by a sliding panel. The schoolyard hundreds of yards away was clearly visible. On a table lay a radio control device.

Suddenly the door was thrown open and the two agents moved in, their backs to the wall, their weapons outstretched.

"Freeze!" shouted David. "O.N.E." He held his gun in one hand, his photo ID in the other.

The three men reacted quickly and it was obvious they were as well trained as David and Thorold. A shot was fired, just missing Smith, and a moment later, Thorold blasted the shotgun, killing the gunman instantly.

The two other men fired their own weapons as they sought cover while Thorold and David shifted and returned the fire, bullets ricocheting everywhere. The computer screen exploded and the light fixtures were blown out. Thorold switched to his handgun.

One of the men threw himself to the floor and rolled toward an exit, shooting wildly until the clip was empty. He jammed another into the handle, using a flurry of bullets for cover. The other raced up a back stairwell as David fired at him rapidly. His rounds struck the stairs, sending up splinters.

Thorold knew the drill: shots had been fired, one man down, and two others moving in opposite directions. They should radio for backup and wait until the building was surrounded and all exits sealed off. But the drill would have to wait. Their adrenaline pumping, they nodded to one another, David heading for the stairwell and Thorold moving to where the other man had disappeared.

David, his back to the staircase wall and his gun stretched out ahead of him, heard the gunman running to the next level. A door opened and shut, and with no idea what lay ahead, he should have stayed back. But it was too late to worry about that now, even as he realized that Thorold might have been right about the Haters. Maybe they had been set up.

"I think you understand my precarious position, Agent Smith," he heard a familiar voice suddenly say. "You did some excellent detective work to find this place. I must congratulate you. Perhaps you will even be buried with a medal." A figure stepped from the shadows up ahead, the figure of Len Parker, a gun in his hand.

"Mr. Parker," David cried in shock. "No! You don't understand. I . . ."

Parker fired the first round straight into David's chest

and he fell back against the wall, his mouth agape, his eyes blank. Parker's second shot was through David's skull. "I'm afraid," he sneered, "that you're the one who doesn't understand."

Chapter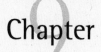

FOR A MOMENT THOROLD THOUGHT of going back. Something was wrong, terribly wrong. His place was with his partner, where together they could handle one man and worry about the other one later, each covering the other's back. They shouldn't have split up like that, not without other backup available.

Thorold waited, trying to slow his breathing, and listened as the other man did the same. He knew he had to make a move soon, so he fired two wild rounds into the room and rushed in, firing again as he spotted his assailant. The man was now holding an automatic rifle, and let loose with a burst of bullets that struck the wall behind Thorold. The gunfire echoed through the room, a cacophony of death as Thorold fired again and retreated back around the corner, praying he was behind a wall thick enough to provide cover.

Thorold counted to himself. *One, two, three, four, five . . .* then looked around the corner, fired, and retreated as another burst of bullets erupted. He moved out again, but when he started to return fire he discovered his weapon was empty. Smiling, his attacker aimed more carefully as Thorold scrambled back to cover behind a stack of crates against a far wall. He kept moving, expecting at any minute to feel the searing pain of a bullet entering his body, but as he reached the crates, he heard a clicking sound behind him. Now they were both out of bullets.

It was then that Thorold spotted the gun on the floor that had been dropped by the man he had killed. Before he could run to it, however, the weapon shook slightly, then flew across the room and into the hand of his attacker. Before he could process what had just occurred, the attacker fired again, and he jumped behind the crates as bullets whistled around him.

Momentarily hidden from view, Thorold climbed onto the crates as the man moved forward boldly, making no attempt to find cover. Partway up the stack, at least ten feet off the ground, Thorold reached into his pocket and pulled out the DNA detector. He hurled it across the room, hoping to momentarily distract the gunman, who only laughed at the desperate attempt. It was then that he heard the deep rumbling sound as Thorold dislodged one of the crates, sending it down on the gunman. And leaping to the ground, he scrambled toward his assailant, who had been knocked to the floor.

Taking the gun from his hand and twisting the man's arm behind his back, he pushed his head against the floor and knocked him unconscious. Yanking the cuffs from the back of his belt, he locked the man's wrists together and, breathing heavily, pulled him from under the crate, then began going through his pockets. It was in the gunman's jacket that he found what he was looking for: a small electronic device with a collapsible antenna and a detonating button.

"A detonator," said Thorold, breathing hard. "So you set up the Haters. They didn't blow up any bus. It was you." He continued searching the pockets of the unconscious man, looking for identification. He pulled out a police-issue folding case with a badge on one side and a photo card on the other, complete with fingerprints and description. "You're working for O.N.E.?" he gasped, staring at the unconscious man, frightened for the first time. Dragging his assailant to a wall with an exposed pipe, he cuffed him there and reloaded his handgun, found the DNA detector he had thrown, turned it on and moved around the room. Seeing that there were no other threats, he started back toward the stairs where his partner had gone. As he reached the top of the stairs and opened the door he saw the sprawled, bloody body of his partner and friend. There would be time for grieving later, time for righteous anger. At the moment all he knew for certain was that he was in a game of cat and mouse and the cats had the upper hand.

He looked up and found himself face-to-face with Len Parker, a gun in his hand. Thorold raised his own weapon. "Overlord Parker, sir," he said. "I'm going to have to ask you to drop that."

There was a smile on Parker's face, a look of utter unconcern. "What tipped you off, Agent Stone? What led you here?" he asked.

"Drop it, Mr. Parker," said Thorold, ignoring the question. "Drop it right now!"

"You're in way over your head, my friend," said Parker quietly.

"Why are you doing this?" asked Thorold. "Why are you setting up the Haters? Why is the O.N.E. lying to the world?"

Parker was silent for a moment, then slowly raised his gun in Thorold's direction. Instinctively, Thorold fired.

Nothing happened. He heard the explosion, felt the kick of the weapon, and saw the smoke belch from the muzzle. But that was it, as if he were firing blanks.

Shaken, Thorold steadied himself and fired again and again, but it was as if each bullet vanished after leaving the chamber.

With the clip empty, Thorold lowered his weapon, certain now that he was about to die. "Who are you?" he asked quietly. "What are you?"

Parker spoke softly, his voice now strangely distant, deeper and more resonant, as if rising from the depths of hell and filling the room with its power. "I am a servant of the Messiah," he proclaimed, "here to rid the world of anyone and everyone who stands in the way. That includes you, Agent Stone."

Parker raised his weapon and fired and Thorold was thrown back by the impact. Dropping to the floor, he lay unmoving, mouth agape, eyes wide, while Parker turned and walked purposely toward the brick wall, passing through it as though it were thin air and not bricks and mortar.

Thorold lay stunned on the floor then rolled agonizingly

on his side and felt for the wound. He touched his breast pocket and realized the bullet had struck the DNA detector, shattering it, but deflecting the bullet. Carefully standing, he stared at the place where Parker had disappeared. Pushing his hands against the brick, he realized the wall was real, not an illusion, and he found the indentations where the bullets had struck. He thought they had disappeared, but they had really passed through the target harmlessly, yet with enough force to shatter the brick behind him.

He carefully looked for a hidden switch, a loose brick or some evidence that the wall was hinged, anything to show him that Len Parker had vanished through a secret door. But there was nothing. Thorold had seen Len Parker pass through solid brick.

In shock, Thorold walked to the body of David Smith, dropping to his knee and lowering his head. Forcing himself to breathe slowly and not hyperventilate, he leaned over his partner's corpse and said, "You were right, buddy. Macalousso's not the only one doing miracles." He paused, then continued grimly, "I won't let them get away with this, David. First my family and now my best friend. I won't let them get away with this."

He stood, steadying himself as he moved to the stairs, walking as fast as he could to where he had left his prisoner. He stopped, amazed. The man was gone. Only the cuffs remained, one around the pipe, the other sitting empty where the missing man's wrist had been.

Chapter

THE BUILDING WAS AN architectural wonder, twenty-seven stories of steel and glass so futuristic, it seemed as if it could have been launched into space. Built as the corporate headquarters for the multinational media conglomerate created by Franco Macalousso's business interests, the sign at its roof was the most familiar logo in the world—the pyramid-and-eye symbol with the banner for "One Nation Earth" below. Inside, the offices seemed to radiate joy and a sense of new beginnings for people of all races, ages, and walks of life, each thankful for the opportunity to serve the Messiah and the new world he was creating. But beneath the massive skyscraper was another world, one without windows, and access limited to a single elevator and stairwell. High-security holding cells, soundproof interrogation rooms, and other facilities to process the Haters were hidden by a massive steel door that prevented anyone but authorized personnel from coming into the area.

The eighteen members of the Davis congregation were quiet as they walked past a row of holding cells. No longer handcuffed, it was obvious that resistance was futile.

"Another batch of Haters," said the guard, handing the man at the desk a pile of papers. "They've all been processed."

"Don't sound so annoyed, Bill," said the clerk. "Eighteen more Haters locked away means we're eighteen steps closer to world peace."

As the Haters were taken to their cells, an angry man approached, holding a frightened teenage boy by the arm, and escorted by an armed guard.

"He insisted on bringing the boy down here," the guard explained. "I can vouch for him. We go to each other's house to celebrate the arrival of the Messiah."

"It's the boy . . . ," the man growled.

"Dad, please," the teenager pleaded. "Please don't do this."

"Tough love. That's what he needs," insisted the man. "Drugs. Alcohol. Christianity. It's all the same. When a boy goes astray, the punishment has to be swift and sure. It's the only way he'll learn."

"Are you saying your son is one of the Haters?" asked the clerk at the booking station.

"Claims to be," said the father. "Has their literature. Sings their songs. His mother and I raised him better but he's been hanging out with a bad lot. He had a Bible in his room. He knows our family's values. We don't allow such obscenity."

"Sir," said the clerk. "I admire your love and respect for our lord and savior, Franco Macalousso, praise his blessed name, but from the looks of him, your son's young. How old is he? Fourteen? Fifteen?"

"Fifteen, but what does that matter?" growled the father. "First the Bible, and tonight, I caught him kneeling by his bed, head bowed, hands clasped together. He said he was thinking about a test coming up at school, but I know better. He wants to be one of the Haters, let him take the consequences."

"But Dad," the boy pleaded. "I was praying for you."

"You're not the first father to turn in a son," the clerk explained. "Probably half the Haters we hold were turned in by family members. It's what we have to do in these times."

The father looked at his son. "I know it may not seem like it right now," he said with a catch in his voice. "I'm doing this for your own good."

The boy's eyes filled with tears. "I'll be okay," he said. "Jesus will protect me and I'll pray for Him to look after you, too."

"What's the matter with you, Joey?" the guard asked angrily. "Can't you see what's going on in this world? Why would you want to be part of a hideous cult like this? We just booked eighteen Haters who blew up a school bus full of kids like you. You keep your nose clean around here. Watch and listen. I think you're going to be glad your dad turned you in."

Suddenly the sound of singing wafted down the hall. The new captives were trying to lift their spirits. "Jesus loves me, this I know, for the Bible tells me so . . ."

Angrily, the guard drew an electric stun gun from his holster, pulled the trigger, and sent a dart connected to the gun by a long, thin wire into the arm of one of the women, the current jolting her body, as she screamed in agony and lost all muscle control.

"Yes, Joey," he continued. "I think this is going to be just what you need."

∽

Len Parker stopped at the newsstand just outside of the O.N.E. building and perused the display racks. Across the top were copies of *Time* magazine, each bearing his photograph on the cover. "Len Parker: One Nation Earth Top Cop" read the banner headline.

He was startled even though he'd known when his picture was being taken that there was talk of a story. There were always pieces being written for placement in some newspaper or magazine. But this was different. *Time* magazine had acted independently to write a story about him. It was his time to shine, and he picked up the magazine to read his life story.

Ever since he was a kid living in one of the poorest, toughest sections of Chicago he had wanted to be a police officer.

Father Mike at Our Lady of Perpetual Devotion, where his mother dragged the family every week, thought Len's interest in law enforcement was a higher calling. The priest had a grandfather and several cousins on the force and often quoted the police motto: "To Protect and to Serve," praising Len for wanting to be a part of that tradition.

But Len's role models were the swaggering street cops

of his neighborhood, the ones who took whatever fruit they wanted from the stands and got envelopes full of cash from bars with illegal backroom joints and meted out justice with a rubber hose. Len wanted that same power, so he watched, listened, and learned, working his way through college in civilian jobs within the department, and going to the academy when he turned twenty-one.

Len learned the system quickly and moved up the chain. He'd work the bars, the brothels, and the drug houses one against the other, and whoever paid him the most stayed open without hassles. But Len also made certain he never collected from the power players, only going to see them when he needed a good word as he moved up the ranks. By the time he was ready to move from city officer to federal cop, he had supporters in place who would do anything for him to keep him from talking. Eventually he had come to the attention of Franco Macalousso, when he was in the United Nations, who elevated him to the top law enforcement position after revealing himself as the Messiah of One Nation Earth.

Now, with his picture on the cover of *Time*, with his ability to take a life at will with no questions asked, he felt like an ancient god elevated to Mt. Olympus, a deity in human form, the Messiah himself.

Smiling, Len Parker walked into the O.N.E. building where a lobby television monitor played the Macalousso-owned WNN, now the voice of One Nation Earth, broadcast in more than one thousand languages and dialects through the world. "Coming up on WNN—Macalousso mania is sweeping the globe," the anchor reported. "Around the world, celebrations continue as citizens of One Nation Earth marvel at the Messiah's latest series of miracles . . ."

Parker entered the elevator and used a key to activate the button for the twenty-seventh floor. The limited access floor, the luxury private office; these, too, set him apart. Len Parker was the most powerful man on earth, next to the Messiah.

"Overlord Parker, sir, we have a problem," said Parker's chief of internal security when he arrived in the office, interrupting his moment of reverie and souring his mood.

"What sort of problem?" he asked, annoyed.

"The second agent, Thorold Stone . . . ," the chief stammered.

"Yes, I'm familiar with Agent Stone," snapped Parker. "I made certain he would cause us no further trouble."

The chief swallowed hard. "Agent Stone is gone. We can't find him."

"What do you mean?" Parker demanded. "I shot him myself. The bullet hit him in the chest." He stared at the chief, clearly stunned. A man with his power should always be fully in control of every situation. He took a deep breath, exhaled slowly, then turned to his underling and said, "Kill him. Find Stone and kill him. Make certain he doesn't escape us again. He knows too much to stay alive."

"Yes, sir," said the chief, "but there's something more, sir."

Parker glared at him, and considered taking out his gun and shooting the man. No one would dare question his action. But it was wrong to kill the messenger. He had to stay calm. "What is it?" He sighed.

"The CD, sir," replied the chief. "We strip-searched all eighteen of the Haters and we checked every inch of the warehouse as well as their homes, offices, and cars. The CD is still missing. Perhaps our intelligence information was wrong. Maybe that preacher didn't have it."

Parker sneered. "Oh, he had it, all right. He worked for me, the lying Hater. He knew all about it, pretending to love the Messiah as much as we do. Then he stole it from me. He stole it and still has it somewhere."

"We'll recheck our steps and widen the search, sir," said the quaking chief.

"You do that," said Parker ominously. "You find it or I swear I'll charge you with being an accessory. The Day of Wonders is less than seventy-two hours away. If that CD makes its way into the wrong hands, if those Haters manage to find out what's on it, they'll do everything they can to expose the Messiah's master plan."

The chief started to speak, then thought better of it. Len Parker seemed barely in control. The man was too dangerous to cross. "I understand," he murmured.

"No, I don't think you do," said Parker angrily. "If you did, you'd have found the disc already."

Chapter

11

HAD THOROLD STONE BEEN THINKING more clearly, he would have stolen a car to make the trip home. Even being there was more of a risk than he should be taking, but there was nowhere else to go even though the homing device on the O.N.E. agent's car was certain to reveal his location. All they had to do was punch in the vehicle's code number and he would be pinpointed in a matter of seconds.

The television was on when Thorold entered, a carryover from his training that had taught him the sound meant that someone was home. This time, however, Thorold was sorry it was on. The stories were all about Macalousso, and for the moment, he did not like to think that a Messiah, a real Messiah, could be so naive about the actions of his underlings.

"A look at the new Europe," said the newscaster as Thorold glanced at the set. "Not since the days of the Holy Roman Empire has the continent found such peace and unity. Without a single shot being fired, Europe, under the leadership of the Messiah, Franco Macalousso, once again rules the world."

The camera switched to the pyramid-and-eye logo of One Nation Earth, then dissolved into a seemingly endless row of poles, each with the flag of a different nation unfurling, as a voice intoned, "One World. One Network. This is WNN."

"Coming up this hour," the anchor continued, "we will be looking at the incredible transformation of the Middle East in the wake of the seven-year peace treaty between Israel and her neighbors. Meanwhile, construction continues on the Temple of Mankind in Jerusalem as One Nation Earth officials are confident that the expected crowds can be managed. But first, our lead story: Another Hater strike has shocked the world. More than seven hundred elderly patients at a veterans hospital near Rome are now confirmed dead in this latest attack by Christian extremists."

"Yeah, right," muttered Stone. "And Santa Claus steals toys."

Thorold stared at the chaos that passed for his work area, trying to decide what he needed to take with him. The desk was covered with papers, books, video- and audiotapes. A personal computer sat next to three VCRs in a rack arrangement, along with a television monitor, a duplicating deck, and mounted speakers.

The walls were covered with newspaper clippings related to the coming of Franco Macalousso, with headlines that read, "Messiah's Miracle Saves World." "Messiah Arrives; Nukes Vanish in Flight." "A New Beginning: 187 Million Enemies of Peace Vaporized." "A Last Message of Hate." "Haters Block Spiritual Breakthrough." "Messiah Heals 7,000 in Athens." "If Not God, Who?"

There were also photos of his academy graduating class, the ceremony when he joined O.N.E.'s enforcement division, and he and Wendy on their honeymoon. Thorold stopped to pick up a photograph of his family smiling happily. "I'll never stop loving you," he whispered, lingering to look at the four of them longer than he should.

Putting the picture on top of a notebook computer, he pulled it from its bay and set it by the door, then hurried to his gun closet where he removed a small revolver and ankle holster along with an automatic and several clips of ammunition for the police issue weapon.

Finally he went to the bookshelf, searching for a book he had purchased out of curiosity, thinking it might be fun to read some day. But now its title—*Aliens Among Us?*—seemed deadly serious after what he had seen Len Parker do at the warehouse. He would read it when he got somewhere safe.

It was then that he heard a noise in what should have been an empty house. He pressed the "mute" button on the TV remote and listened closely to the sound of creaking floorboards. Someone else was in the house and as he moved swiftly to where he had left his weapons, an O.N.E. agent emerged from the shadows holding a gun.

"Freeze, Stone," he ordered. "Get your hands up where I can see them."

"Those Haters didn't blow up that bus," said Thorold. He recognized the agent as part of the team that worked for Len Parker, and knew only too well his lethal mission. But if he could distract him, if he could get him talking . . .

"That doesn't matter," the agent snapped. "They're still Haters. If they didn't do it, they did something else. They're all alike."

"No," insisted Thorold. "They were set up by Parker and you're helping him."

The agent sneered. "Let's just say I'm keeping attention focused on the Haters, where it should be. Now get your hands up above your head."

Thorold shrugged, then slowly started moving his hands. The agent took his weapon in a two-handed grip, preparing to fire, when Thorold released the mute on the remote control that was still in his hands. The sudden loud sound from the television startled the agent, who swung around, accidentally firing a round into the wall as he did.

Thorold leaped at him, grabbing his wrist with both hands, struggling for the gun, then raised his knee and brought the man's arm sharply down on it, breaking the bone. The agent dropped the gun, screaming in pain, and Thorold delivered a blow into his stomach with his elbow then punched him twice more in the gut, grabbing him by the collar and smashing him into the wall, where he fell to the ground unconscious, the weight of his body triggering a broadcast button on the radio he had in his pocket to stay in contact with headquarters.

The brutality of his action surprised Thorold, who thought of himself as basically a peaceful man. But what he had done to the agent was vicious, and as he looked at the unconscious figure on the ground, he realized the stress of the past several hours was becoming too much for him. Was

he turning into one of the predators, a man as evil as Len
Parker? "Agent Dempsey . . . Agent Dempsey, do you
copy?" came a voice from the unconscious man's lapel.
Thorold realized immediately what had happened. O.N.E.
headquarters had been alerted.

There was no time to think. He had to move, had to act.
He picked up Dempsey's gun, aimed it at the computer
monitor on the desk, and fired a round, exploding the monitor, then stuffed the weapon in his belt and, stepping over
the unconscious agent, grabbed his laptop and the family
photo and hurried out the door.

"All tactical units in the vicinity of 357 Park," the radio
squawked behind him. "Cross street Lawn; we have a possible 721. Suspect is armed and dangerous."

Thorold could hear the sirens as he raced to his car.
And he knew he had no more than a minute before units
would begin arriving. Tossing the computer into the car, he
shot backward out of the drive, away from the louder of the
two sirens he was hearing in the distance.

Turning right at the corner, left at the next, he pulled
into the drive of a house with a "For Sale" sign on the lawn.
He drove around to the garage in the back and, breathing
hard, sat in the car with the engine running and the gun on
the seat next to him. It was then he remembered the homing device still in his car.

Thorold got out, taking the computer and family photo
with him. He checked one car after another along the block,
running his hand around the inside of the bumpers, looking for spare keys in small metal key safes that he knew

many suburbanites used. It was on his sixth try that he found what he was after and removing the key, he quietly opened the car door and started the engine, driving onto the street and speeding into the twilight.

Chapter

WHAT THOROLD STONE NEEDED, he thought, was a fifteen-year-old kid. He had been using computers for years and had been given additional training when he joined the One Nation Earth. Yet as simple a task as getting a CD to play on his laptop was beyond him. The silver disc Davis had hidden in the book looked like a regulation compact disc, but his machine wouldn't read it. Perhaps some teenage hacker might be able to help him.

He thought about going to a shopping mall, and setting up his machine on one of the benches, pretending to work as the kids milled around. Eventually one of them might come by and help him play the CD.

But Thorold Stone was a wanted man. He knew that Len Parker would stop at nothing to hunt down a special agent in the Messiah's own enforcement agency who had doubts about who Franco Macalousso really was. The Haters were easy targets. But to have an elite member of the Messiah's security forces claim that Macalousso was a fraud was intolerable. Alive, Thorold Stone could do more damage to the Messiah's reputation than any number of Haters, which was why he had to lay low and avoid all public places, even shopping malls. Any special agent spotting him would have ordered to shoot to kill.

Abandoning the mall idea, Thorold drove to an electronics store in a remote part of the city. A bell sounded as Thorold entered the store, but the sound was all but drowned out by the voice of Franco Macalousso amplified over and over on two dozen television sets along one wall. "But remember this," he proclaimed. "I have come to save you. Not just your earthly bodies, as I did when I removed your terrible weapons of mass destruction, but your heavenly bodies as well." The effect was frightening as Macalousso seemed to be an all-seeing, all-pervasive presence. Thorold tried to ignore the televised speech as he walked to the computer section and looked over the different machines.

"And in order to save your souls," Macalousso continued, "I have had to remove those who stood in the way. Now it is time to move forward into a new world of wonders."

Thorold found a demonstration computer and checked the specifications. It was obviously state of the art, and he quietly inserted the CD.

"This world of wonders is unlike anything you have ever imagined," said the two dozen Macaloussos. "Things that until now have been hidden will be revealed. Things of darkness will be shown the light."

It was a speech Thorold had heard before. The Day of Wonders was to be the biggest event the planet had ever seen, but if creatures of darkness fear the light, he wondered who would be exposed if the light of truth were ever to be ignited.

"Can I help you, sir?" asked a salesclerk, startling him as she approached from behind.

Relax, he told himself. *Relax.* "I didn't notice you," he said, forcing himself to smile. "I . . ."

"Sorry," said the clerk. "I didn't mean to startle you. You looked so preoccupied with our Millennium 2120 I thought you might need some help."

"No. That's okay. I don't really . . ." *Take a deep breath. Exhale. She's trying to earn her pay, she's not the enemy,* he told himself. "I've been considering this model for some time," he said. "But a problem came up."

"We handle our own financing if that will help," she said. "Ninety days same as cash."

"The cost isn't the problem," he replied. "I was given a CD, and since I'm buying the latest model I thought I'd pop it in the drive and see what came up on the screen. But it gives me an error reading."

The salesclerk took the CD from the drive and studied it for a moment. "This isn't your normal CD," she said. "It could have been written on a special CD-ROM machine, maybe an experimental model. That's unlikely, though. It's probably a proprietary CD."

"What does that mean?" he asked.

"It has a special security encoding unique to one computer," she replied. "You have to have the computer that wrote it in order to read it. Do you know where it came from?"

"I . . . I got it from . . . a friend of mine," he stammered. "I can't imagine she'd give me a CD like that. Is there someone else on the staff who might be able to . . ."

But the salesclerk was no longer listening. Instead she was staring at the bank of television monitors, her face ashen, her mouth agape. Thorold turned and saw his face on screen after screen. Underneath, in large letters, were the words WANTED FOR MURDER.

Thorold cursed. They weren't going to quietly take care of one of their own as he anticipated. He was now the subject of a manhunt.

"O.N.E. officials are looking for Thorold Stone, a Hater responsible for blowing up a school bus earlier today," a news anchor reported.

It was worse than he thought. They were framing him for the school bus incident, branding him as a Hater and hoping for vigilante justice, depending on some radical Macalousso follower to serve as executioner.

"Thorold Henry Stone reportedly left a note in his office confessing not only to this blatant act of terrorism but also to killing his partner and longtime friend, David Smith. Citizens are warned . . ."

"It's him!" the clerk screamed. "The one on television. Call the police! Call the police!"

Thorold grabbed the CD out of the salesclerk's hand and turned and ran down the aisles blindly bumping into people and careening off displays. A young store employee stepped in front of him, but Thorold pushed him off balance, opened the door, and ran to his car. He would have to assume the license had been spotted and that he would have to steal another one and keep running until he knew what was on the CD and what it might mean.

⁓

Thorold had found a station wagon left running outside a post office and although he felt badly about taking the car, he knew he had no choice. He had to find a way to read the CD. If he could stay alive long enough to make use of the data . . .

Thorold drove into a rural area where he and Wendy had taken their children for picnics. Exhausted, he parked the car behind a roadside billboard featuring Franco Macalousso's face and the words, "The Day of Wonders is for all of us. Do your part. Report Haters." It seemed adequate cover for the world's newest "Hater," he thought ironically.

Desperate to solve the mystery of the CD, Thorold worked on his laptop one more time, inserting the CD and trying every way he knew to access the drive. But the screen always announced the same message "Unable to read the file." Finally he shut down the computer and set it on the seat next to him as he picked up the photo of his family, and risked turning on the interior light long enough to take another look at Wendy and the children. He slumped back against the seat, giving in to the overwhelming fatigue.

Thorold slept fitfully, moving in and out of dreams, finding himself back in the warehouse beside Elder Davis. Others were there including the rest of the congregation, David and the SWAT team, yet all were in shadows, as though they were all onstage with only Davis and Thorold in spotlights.

"It's perfectly clear to anyone who's not afraid to open

up a Bible," said David, his words like a loving rebuke, a parent arguing with a stubborn child.

"I heard enough of this Bible prophecy nonsense from my wife," Thorold was saying in his dream. "And look where it got her."

Davis gradually faded from view to be replaced by Wendy. "It got us to heaven, Thorold," she whispered.

He reached out to embrace his wife, but instead found himself holding his handgun, firing at Len Parker and watching the bullet leave the barrel in slow motion, and move effortlessly toward Parker, heading directly for the kill zone. But the bullet never reached Parker, instead fading from existence.

Angry that Parker had taken Wendy from him, Thorold fired again and again, until the weapon was empty. But Parker simply stood there, smiling and unharmed. Enraged, Thorold heaved his gun and started to charge, only to find himself cradling the dying David Smith. "The answer's on that disc, Thorold," he groaned. "It's all up to you."

David's body vanished, leaving Thorold on his knees staring at a gun on the warehouse floor. As he watched, he saw the gun vibrate then move quickly across the floor, as if in an invisible game of shuffleboard. Rising from the ground, it landed in the hand of a grinning terrorist who took careful aim and pulled the trigger. Thorold lunged forward, knocking the terrorist over and wrestling him to the ground. Then suddenly, his arms were empty, his enemies vanished, leaving him alone in a desolate dreamscape.

The sound of a blaring car horn jolted Thorold awake.

He had leaned onto the steering wheel, sounding the horn, and shattering his sleep. He sat up, with his back aching, his neck stiff, and looked around trying to remember where he was and why. Looking down at the seat he glanced at the photo of his family, then picked up the CD. Staring at it for a few moments, he wished he could will it to work for him. "I almost died for you," he said to the CD, as though it were alive. "If it hadn't been for that DNA detector . . ."

And then Thorold remembered the stories he had heard in the squad room about the scientist who had developed the device. "That guy can do things with a computer that would blow your mind," David had once told him.

Willy . . . Thorold remembered. Willy Holmes. That was his name.

Chapter

THE HOUSE WAS ON A NONDESCRIPT STREET of two- and three-bedroom houses that over the years had become a cohesive community. A neighborhood of young families and retirees. Among the houses was one distinguished only by a wheelchair ramp at the front door: 668 Waverly, the home of Willy Holmes. A sign on the front door advised, BEWARE OF DOG and beneath that, in smaller letters, were the words "He's small but he knows Kung Fu." Smiling despite his stress, Thorold opened the screen and raised a heavy knocker. But before he could use it, a series of gunshots echoed inside the house. Drawing his gun, he grabbed the door handle, found it unlocked, and quietly pushed open the door. Moving swiftly into the hallway he was stopped by the sound of more shots being fired, seemingly coming from the back of the house. Moving to the right, Thorold entered the sparsely furnished living room toward a door to one side. He flattened his back against the wall as he opened it then heard a voice drawling, "Well, I'll tell you, pilgrim. We don't have room for hombres like you around these parts."

Thorold recognized the accent, a very bad John Wayne imitation and as he stood, confused, there was one final shot.

Thorold stepped inside, and found himself confronted by Willy Holmes, dressed like a kid at a Halloween party in a white cowboy suit with a ten-gallon hat, fringed shirt, gun belt, and surprisingly small cowboy boots on his shriveled legs. A small dog was running around his wheelchair, jumping and yipping as its tail wagged furiously.

The electronics expert had a large pair of high-tech goggles over his eyes and a silver revolver in his hand. There was a small receiver pack and antenna attached to the goggles and the revolver had a thin wire running down from its grip to an elaborate, handmade device. The room was crowded with an array of highly sophisticated computers, electronic testing devices, miniature tools, microchips, circuit boards, and contraptions Thorold had never seen before. It was obviously a well-equipped laboratory, arranged for the ease of a man trapped in a wheelchair.

Suddenly, Willy spun the chair around and aimed his revolver at Thorold.

"Whoa there, partner, I come in peace!" Thorold exclaimed, not sure if Willy could even see him through the goggles.

Startled, the scientist shouted, "Who are you?" and raised his goggles.

"Thorold Stone," he replied. "Is that gun real?"

"Is yours?" the man shot back.

"I'm sorry," said Stone, putting the weapon back in its holster. "I heard the gunshots and thought . . ."

"The gunshots were real," Willy explained. "They are digital recordings I made at a firing range." Pausing for a moment, he said, "You're the one who killed David Smith, aren't you?" There was no fear in his voice, just a question from someone who had long ago realized that there was little more life could do to him than it had already done, an attitude that made him fearless and direct.

"David was my friend!" Thorold replied angrily.

Willy's face was somber as he studied the fugitive. "If he was your friend, why is he dead?"

"We ran into what we thought were terrorists," Thorold explained. "I killed one, but they got David."

"Then why are they saying that you're wanted for the murder?" Willy asked.

"They have to say that," Thorold continued. "I recognized the men who did it. Now they're after me."

"And who is it that's trying to set you up?" asked Willy cautiously.

"Len Parker," replied Thorold, watching the man's face for a reaction. But the scientist only signaled for his dog to jump onto his lap. The animal obeyed and Willy petted him, studying Thorold and thinking. "You're saying that the Messiah would authorize murder?" he asked at last.

"I'm saying Len Parker lied. Beyond that, I can tell you that's not the only lie being told. If you'll just give me a few minutes of your time, I'll prove it to you."

"Why should I listen to you?" Willy muttered.

"Because I need your help," Thorold admitted.

"Are you a Hater?" Willy asked.

"I'm a man looking for the truth," Thorold answered. "I have no other place to turn."

"And if I say no?" Willy asked, adding, "You know this gun is real."

"Yes, but somehow I think you won't use it," Thorold said with a smile.

"Don't tempt me," quipped the scientist.

⚮

The system was brutally effective, aiming to keep the Haters in small clusters, letting them keep their foolish prayers and songs to the false one who came before the Messiah, only to separate them at the right time, psychologically if possible, with violence if necessary. Alone, helpless, and in terror, the truly faithful would die and the weak ones could be used to subvert the others.

Not that Len Parker cared how they were disposed of. They were fools for clinging to their Bibles and their stories of the weakling who hung on a cross. They had nothing to offer One Nation Earth.

Even those whom torture could convince were not people to be trusted. They would speak the name of Jesus one day, and the name of the Messiah the next, worshiping the statue of a howling dog if they were frightened enough. Their only purpose was to undermine the will of their fellow Haters. He would let them parade around as examples of the Messiah's love, then quietly eliminate them. And now it was time to deal with the Davis congregation. There would be no mercy for the man who was their leader, a serious convert after the day of the Disappeared. He would certainly die praising his false god, joyously sharing the pain of the one he called his savior. Such people were cancerous growths on society; they must be crushed before they infected others.

Davis's wife; however, was something else. She had worked for the One Nation Earth staff during high-level planning for the Day of Wonders. She may not have known the details, but she had access to all the materials being prepared. It was even possible that it was she who had stolen the CD and passed it along to her husband, with no idea of the importance of the disc.

What mattered was that Anna Davis had worked for the Messiah employed at One Nation Earth headquarters. A Hater who, under the right pressure, might reveal their underground network. All he needed was the right balance of terror, isolation, and pain.

Parker walked down the corridor of holding cells with two uniformed guards. They passed various Haters, their lips silently moving in prayer or their faces filled with disdain. But those who had experienced his methods moved to the farthest corner of their cells, huddled in wide-eyed terror.

The Davis prisoners showed none of these reactions. They were too new to know what could happen, too trusting to believe their lives could be in danger. Elder Davis had even given his name as "Paul" when being booked, saying he was sharing the prison experience of one of the earliest leaders in the young Jesus movement.

A guard opened the cell, the other stepping inside and grabbing Mrs. Davis, who did not resist.

"No! She has done nothing. I am the one you want," cried her husband. He had been ready to pick up the cross and follow Jesus, but the thought of being left behind in the cell was inconceivable. He stepped in front of the guard and grabbed his wrist, unaware that Len Parker had drawn a gun from his pocket.

"No, Daddy! No!" shouted the pastor's daughter, but it was too late. Len Parker fired a single round into Davis's chest. He stepped back, his mouth moving but no sound coming out, staring at his wife and daughter, then sinking to his knees, clutching the wound. Slowly, painfully, he found the strength to speak the words, "I love you." Blood gushed from his mouth as he fell forward. "I'll be waiting," he whispered.

Mrs. Davis shook off the guard and took her dying husband in her arms, cradling his head and kissing him. Tears came to her eyes, yet when she looked at Len Parker, it seemed more in pity than hate.

"Murderers!" screamed the daughter. "You killed my daddy."

"Leave him!" snapped Parker, nodding to the guard. "Take this hysterical teenager out of here."

Reaching for the girl, the guard's face was raked by her fingernails. He gripped her arm, twisting it around against the back of her shoulder, and forced her to her knees as she continued screaming, then brought his knee sharply against her throat. She dropped, frantically gulping for air. The guard kneeled down, lifting her onto his shoulder, and carried her from the cell. As he moved down the corridor,

Parker looked at Mrs. Davis and sneered. "It's been a while since you left One Nation Earth, Mrs. Davis, and I've been most interested in talking with you. I had a few hours free on my schedule today, so I thought I'd drop by to see you. I hope we haven't caught you at a bad time."

To Parker's surprise, Anna Davis's voice was soft and controlled even though her face was filled with anguish. "Leave my daughter out of this," she said. "She hasn't done anything to you. My husband and I are the ones you wanted. Just leave her be. She's only a child."

Parker looked at the woman silently, as if seriously considering her request. Then he smiled and said, "She won't be a child for long."

Only then did the woman before him begin to scream.

Chapter 14

THEY HAD BEEN TALKING for more than an hour and no matter what Willy may have thought of Thorold, it was clear the scientist was an intensely lonely man. The close attention of another human was a rare treat, even if his visitor might be a dangerous killer.

They sat at a table, drinking coffee while Willy smoked a cigarette. "Nasty habit," Willy told him when he lit another from the ember of the last. "Doctor says they'll stunt my growth." He laughed with a wheezing sound.

The two men had become more relaxed as they talked, Willy not only listening closely to what Thorold said, but asking questions that probed at the truth.

"So the Haters weren't responsible for the school bus, orphanage, or old-age home bombings?" Willy asked.

"None of it," was Thorold's emphatic reply.

"And in this last one, you say you personally saw Len Parker in the warehouse where the bomb was triggered?"

"Yes," answered Thorold. "He killed my partner and he would have killed me if that DNA detector you made hadn't deflected the bullet."

"Truly a noble piece of electronics." Willy smiled. "But it's supposed to find people, not save them from bullets."

Willy stared at the agent, thinking, saying nothing. Then, softly, he asked, "Why?"

"Why what?" asked Thorold.

"Why Len Parker? Why One Nation Earth? Why anything connected with Franco Macalousso?" asked the scientist. "You saw the same news coverage I did, that day in Megiddo. How could such a man . . ." He paused, searching for the words. "Want to kill Christians?" Thorold asked softly.

"Yes."

"I don't know," Thorold admitted. "I can't explain Franco Macalousso. All I know is that we've been lied to about the Haters. And if O.N.E. is lying to us about that, then who knows what else they might be lying about? If Macalousso is deceiving us, he can't be who he says he is. You can't be God and a liar."

"Wait a minute!" protested Willy. "You can say what you want about Len Parker and anyone else in O.N.E. They're humans, and humans have always corrupted themselves in the name of power and money. But the Messiah? What makes you think he knows anything about this?"

"Look at this logically," Thorold insisted. "We had miracles that everyone witnessed and we were all overwhelmed by them. The man saved the planet from obliteration.

"The way I see it, Willy, anyone who can do what he did has nothing to fear from anyone. If he's really the

Messiah, why does he need the big police agency, the inter-rogation rooms, the SWAT teams? Why can't he just vapor-ize his enemies? I can't believe that a god would need someone like Len Parker. I don't think a god would be fomenting hate."

"So what do you think?" Willy demanded. "You're the great investigator. Who do you think this guy is?'

"Someone from another planet," Thorold ventured. "Macalousso, Parker, all of them."

Willy laughed. "Okay, the Messiah's a space alien and I'm a long-distance runner."

"But what's a better explanation," demanded Thorold, "that he's Satan? Look, I saw bullets strike Len Parker with no effect. I saw him walk through a wall. I have seen things with my own eyes I can't believe."

"And so have I," said Willy. "You walked in when I was having a shoot-out at the OK Corral. I saw everyone, smelled everything. When I shot them, they went down just like when I was a kid playing cowboys. Only now I can walk across the prairie, ride a horse, kick the gun out of a bad guy's hand. You saw it, didn't you?"

"I saw you wearing goggles and some sort of electronic gadget on your head," replied Thorold.

"Those goggles brought me an illusion as lifelike as what you saw," explained Willy. "What we think we see is not necessarily what is real."

"What I saw was not some virtual reality contraption," insisted Thorold.

Willy looked sadly at the agent. "What I want to know

is why it's easier for you to think Franco Macalousso is an alien than to believe he's God."

"Because I don't know if there's life on other planets, but I do know there's no God," answered Thorold. "Look, I didn't come here for a philosophical discussion. I think the answer I'm looking for is on the disc." He pulled it from his pocket and handed it to Willy.

"It's an O.N.E. disc all right," said Willy, looking it over. "It will fit on a standard CD-ROM, but it won't show you anything. You need a special drive and code access," he said as he wheeled himself to one of many computers in the room and inserted the disc.

Thorold watched the monitor until a message appeared that read, "O.N.E. internal control. Enter your password."

Willy punched several keys, his fingers flying over the board. "Casement code," read the screen.

"You sure you can do this?" asked Thorold.

"I designed the security graphics myself," replied Willy. He pressed several more keys and the pyramid-and-eye symbol appeared on the screen with the words "Welcome to the Day of Wonders Project. Press any key to continue."

Willy frowned. "This is the project I've been working on. You say the Haters had a copy of this?"

"Yes," answered Thorold. "What is it?"

"It's the Day of Wonders Project," he said.

The screen requested a password and Willy typed in his authorization. "Please type your password," repeated the screen.

Willy shrugged his shoulders and typed in his code

again. Once again it failed to work. Frustrated, his fingers seemed to fly over the keyboard, but he could not break into the disc.

"What's wrong?" asked Thorold.

"Do you realize what this is?" demanded Willy. "It's a new program for the Day of Wonders Virtual World System."

"You said you worked on it," Thorold reminded him. "Why can't you get access to it?"

"My password doesn't work. No password works. They've changed the Interlink system," explained Willy, turning to Thorold. "What do you know about the Day of Wonders?" he asked.

"I know it's being advertised on half the billboards in the city, on the radio and television stations, and in the newspapers," he answered. "It's like a preview of coming attractions to a new movie. It's supposed to be the best day of our lives, the start of something even greater than the day the world was saved."

Willy nodded. "Then you know about as much as everyone else, including me, and I worked on the project. There were a couple dozen of us assigned from around the world. All of us had been in law enforcement. All of us had been hired by One Nation Earth and all of us were given a small piece of coding to develop. We all had special access codes and I created a secret master code that I shared only with Overlord Parker. The Interlink was the key to the way we worked. Each day, we would type a special code that would send our work to Interlink, where it would be stored like a giant jigsaw puzzle. Then Interlink assembled the pieces to create the complete program. A week ago it was done and we were all given access to the finished program so we could troubleshoot."

"Then this equipment should let you play the CD," said Thorold.

"Not exactly," cautioned Willy. "None of us are able to access the entire system. That was being saved for the Day of Wonders. All we could do was reach a single part so we could fix glitches. Interlink is coded to tell when we try to access the full disc. It sends a signal to Overlord Parker when we try to work on different parts, and it shuts down completely. Permission to continue would have to come directly from Parker." He turned back to the computer. "This is a new program. Someone's made extensive modifications to the system. The player still works, and some of the access codes. But that's all."

"Would Len Parker know the full code?" asked Thorold urgently.

"Of course," replied Willy. He would have the key and he answers directly to Bishop Bancroft, who's in charge of the whole Day of Wonders Project. And Bishop Bancroft reports directly to the Messiah."

"Then we'll have to get it from him," said Thorold grimly. "Whatever is going on, something tells me that the Day of Wonders is not going to be the joyous time we keep hearing about."

Chapter 15

ONLY THOSE WHO HAD BEEN THROUGH interrogation understood the ominous nature of the special room that Anna Davis found herself in. The floor was smooth concrete, sloping gently toward a drain in the center, and along one wall hung what looked like a garden hose with an adjustable nozzle to wash away the blood and gore. The walls themselves were covered with seamless material similar to that used in hospital operating rooms for complete cleaning. It was a rather odd place to be questioned, unless the person became stubborn and until something harsher than words had to be used and the blood began to flow . . .

Anna Davis sat on a metal chair, her wrists tied behind her back. Len Parker sat opposite her, straddling the seat, his chin resting on his folded arms, in a posture relaxed and casual as if sharing a conversation with an old friend.

"It seems we've chosen different sides, haven't we, Anna?" His voice was quiet, no different from when he walked by her desk in O.N.E. and exchanged pleasantries. "We're both soldiers hoping to win a war in which only one will prevail."

Anna Davis stared at Parker, her face bruised and swollen, registering no emotion. She had been slapped and punched enough to cause pain, and to let her know that there could be an escalation of abuse if she resisted.

But God had brought her to this point and she would have to trust in the Lord no matter what happened. He would be with her. He would be with them all.

Parker rose from his chair and walked slowly around the small cell. From behind, he touched her shoulder, leaning forward, and speaking in a whisper, "I thought about joining your side once. I was raised in a church, you know. I used to memorize Bible verses and even won prizes when we had contests at the annual church picnic. Yes, I came very close. But do you know why I did not?" Parker resumed walking. "You're living a lie!" he shouted suddenly. "I know what the Bible says. I know Genesis claims that God made us in His image, that Adam and Eve were chastised for seeking the fruit of the tree of the knowledge of good and evil. There is so little difference between God and man: just one piece of fruit. He is so insecure, He wants to keep us from our rightful inheritance." He raised his eyebrows. "Don't look so surprised, Anna. I told you I was raised in the church. I was almost deceived by its lies. I could have been a Hater like one of you, but thank our Messiah, that did not happen. The Messiah opened my eyes and let me see that we can all achieve godhood. Look at what I've become through believing in the world Franco Macalousso has brought to enrich us. That's what God's afraid of. That's why He tries to keep us fearful, humble, and thankful for the crumbs when we could really have the whole loaf. The Messiah has shown us that the power lies within all of us."

"Is it the god within you that allows you to murder a gentle, unarmed man whose only crime was to love his wife?" asked Anna Davis through her bruised and bloodied mouth. "Is it this god within you that allows you to victimize a helpless teenage girl? Is it this god within you that allows you to tie me to a chair, and beat me like a dog? Is that what you have sold your soul for? Cain had such power. So did Pharaoh. So did the father of Salome, who gave his daughter the head of a prophet. Bullies and tyrants and petty little men have always had such power. You're not so special."

"You have not seen the powers with which I have been gifted," thundered Parker. "You have no idea what awaits you unless you denounce the false one and join. Your co-workers, your neighbors, many of your friends have all done this. How could so many upright people be wrong? Are you the only one who sees the truth?"

"I see that God loves the outcast," was her defiant reply. "The person who has the courage to stand alone for His sake. The prophets were all unlikely vessels of His holy Word. They were shunned and scorned, and terrorized by the establishment. Yet God was with them, and because He stood by their side, their words had real power. The way of the cross is a gift of strength, not a sign of weakness. Jesus was murdered. Paul was murdered. Yet the word that was left has spread to prove God's purpose in all the world. Your false Messiah can only triumph by killing those who would only speak against him walking humbly, in truth, and loving the Lord."

Len Parker stepped over to her, slapping her hard across the face. Then, in a calm voice, he said, "So let's try this one more time. Did Thorold Stone join your deluded cause? And what is he planning to do with that CD?"

Mrs. Davis sat quietly. Her arms were beginning to ache in their tethered position, but she knew that any indication of discomfort would be a signal to Parker of weakness.

"Come on," he continued. "Stop playing games with me. I know your husband gave him that disc. Your daughter told us all about it."

This time Anna Davis reacted as Parker had hoped as he touched on overwhelming emotions. Like many teenagers her daughter was belligerent toward those she disliked and if she had talked about the CD, it could only mean they had hurt her in ways Anna didn't want to imagine.

"What have you done with her?" she demanded.

Len Parker ignored the question. "Now I want to know what Stone is planning to do with that CD. I want to know his role in the Haters."

"And I want to know what you have done with my daughter. I will tell you nothing until you answer me," said Anna.

"Stop worrying about your daughter." Parker sneered. "She is in absolutely no pain whatsoever . . ." He paused, looking deeply into the eyes of the woman he considered a traitor to O.N.E. He could see she was frightened now, for the first time. Then, softly, slowly, he added, "She is in no pain . . . now."

With a sound like a high-pitched keening Anna began rocking her body, tears streaming down her face.

"Noooooooooo . . ."

Parker's features were contorted with disgust. "Don't get so upset, Anna," he said. "It's not as if you Haters have rich, full lives ahead of you. You won't even live long enough to see what the Day of Wonders is really all about. A pity, too. Your Mr. Stone has no idea what he's up against. But we know better, don't we, Anna? We know I will do anything I need to get what I want. Now let's talk about Agent Stone. When did he make a decision to join the Haters?"

☙

Thorold sensed a change in Willy's attitude as he became more relaxed and animated, and they talked like two old friends. He was not sure if he had convinced Willy of the truth or if the scientist was so lonely he was grateful for any company, even a wanted criminal.

"So what is this Day of Wonders Project?" Thorold asked.

"Nobody knows exactly," Willy replied.

"But someone with your genius, someone who designed the security system, must have an idea," Thorold pressed.

"Maybe an idea, but I don't know anything about the final program," Willy admitted.

"There have been test versions," he continued. "We checked for sound, for graphics, for neural response. We also tested concepts like the virtual reality equipment you found me wearing, which may have seemed like just a computer game but was really quite a bit more. It's light-years ahead of what we thought was possible before the Messiah revealed himself." He wheeled himself toward a platform in the middle of the room, crossing to an elaborate console. Turning on the power, he made adjustments on a computer keyboard. "Pick up the goggles on the left. I'll use another pair," instructed Willy.

"Select Desired Virtual World," prompted the on-screen menu that flashed in front of their eyes with the choices "OK Corral, Aspen Ski Challenge, Climbing Everest, Olympic Games, Walk on the Beach." Selecting "Walk on the Beach," Willy said, "You don't realize how far Macalousso's taken us. What you're going to experience is unlike anything you've ever seen."

Thorold Stone put on his goggles and took a deep breath, his lungs filling with the moist, warm air as a breeze came across the beach of a vast ocean. He was barefoot, in swim trunks, and he could feel the sand between his toes and the sun shining warmly on his body. In front of him was Willy Holmes, no longer in his chair, his body powerful from regular exercise.

Thorold reached up and lifted the goggles, wondering if he had somehow been transported to a real beach. But he still was in the room and Willy still was in his wheelchair. Startled, Thorold lowered the goggles over his eyes and was back on the beach again where Willy was spreading sun-block on his body. "Lotion?" he asked casually, holding the tube up to Thorold.

"Do I need it?" Thorold asked. Wherever he was, whatever was happening, he was ready to believe anything was possible.

"Not really," Willy said. "I'm just a big fan of ambience."

"This is so real," murmured Thorold. "I mean, I can feel the water, smell it. If I had one of these, I'd never leave the house."

Willy quietly replied, "If I didn't have one of these, I'd never leave my chair." He began moving down the beach, signaling for Thorold to join him. As they moved and splashed in the waves, Thorold wondered when they would reach the end of the cord that connected the goggles to the computer processor. "How can we do this?" he asked. "The wire to the goggles can't be more than ten feet."

"Your legs aren't moving," Willy explained. "Your muscles are being stimulated by a small electrical current. You can run ten miles along this beach feeling every step of the way. Your breathing will change and your heart will pump. Yet if you take off your goggles, you'll find you haven't moved a foot."

"All this technology came from Macalousso. He's far beyond where we were in our development. Your brain literally can't tell the difference between this and reality."

"I've been around computers all my life, but this stuff is beyond my wildest dreams."

Both men ducked as a bird swooped in low to catch a fish.

"Actually, it is my wildest dream," Willy continued. "Everything is exactly how I imagined a perfect world to be."

"How far can you go with this?" asked Thorold.

"My guess is you can have anything you can imagine. I can even see prisons using the technology with uncontrollable criminals, letting them commit all the crime they want safely locked in a cell. It's like living out your dreams."

"I wouldn't want to be living the dreams I've been having," said Thorold ruefully.

"Lost loved ones?" asked Willy sympathetically. "Some of the Disappeared?"

"Yes," admitted Thorold. He noticed a stone lying on the sand. He picked it up and chucked it across the water. "But I know that everyone lost someone. We were all touched by that day. My wife was a believer. She would be classed as a Hater if she were still . . . here. I loved her. I still love her. I know I should get past it, especially with the tragedies I've seen others trying to overcome, but I just can't seem to forget her." He paused, turning to the scientist. "What about you, Willy? Who did you lose?"

"My grandmother and my sister," Willy replied sadly. "Sis practically raised me, even when she started her career as a television anchor. She used to call me all the time when she had to travel on a story. My grandmother was one of those Holy Joes, always looking at the bright side of things. Called my legs a blessing. She said that they were God's way of guiding me to my true gift. She said that one day I would understand. But I miss her. I miss them both."

Thorold nodded. "When I found out that Parker was setting up Haters, it was the first glimmer of hope I've had since the vanishings. Suddenly, for the first time, there was something to hold on to. Maybe my wife wasn't some evil person after all. Maybe she was just . . . different, better, more insightful. I don't know. Good people are a threat sometimes just because they refuse to go along with what they think is wrong. I figured my wife and kids were dead. Now I'm not so certain. If I can prove Macalousso knew about all this, that he's been lying about it, maybe I can find out what happened to them."

The two men continued walking along the beach, both deep in thought. In the distance sailboats moved lazily on the water; birds were flying overhead, and a few white clouds drifted through the blue sky. Looking farther up the beach he saw small children laughing and running and a large dog, barking at birds, racing into the water and pausing only long enough to shake himself off.

"I can't believe this," marveled Thorold. Despite all the dangers and fears of the day, putting on the goggles was like being given a new life, a chance for happiness. "So much for the idea that seeing is believing."

"That's the whole point," exclaimed Willy. "You can't trust your senses when you're in here. That's why I like it. It's a world without responsibilities, a world without consequences. You can do anything and there's no price to be paid."

"What do you mean? Have an affair? Kill someone?" asked Thorold.

"More than that. Watch." Willy walked over to a broken seashell in the sand with a ragged edge, sharp and pointed like a knife. "Give me your arm," he said. Grasping Thorold's wrist, he cut it with the shell, a thin red line forming and blood welling slowly.

Thorold stared at the wound for a moment. "It . . . it's bleeding," he said. "But there's no pain. But the blood is real, isn't it?"

"Take off your goggles," Willy suggested.

Thorold complied, finding everything was as he remembered it, from Willy in his wheelchair to the elaborate computer equipment in the room. He stared at his wrist. There was no hint of injury. "This is incredible," he whispered.

Suddenly the sound of the doorbell startled both Willy and Thorold back to reality. Followed by a pounding on the door. Thorold looked for a place to hide. He thought he had covered his tracks enough to avoid detection, and was certain Willy had no secret alarm to alert O.N.E., but for all he knew, when they had tried to access the Day of Wonders disc, a homing signal had been triggered.

Willy quickly wheeled over to a small black-and-white monitor rigged with exterior surveillance cameras. Looking over his shoulder Thorold saw a deliveryman standing at the door in a World Post uniform.

"Relax. The cavalry hasn't arrived," said Willy, wheeling out of the room to the front door.

"Mr. William W. Holmes?" asked the deliveryman.

"That's me," said Willy.

"I need you to sign for a Day of Wonders package," the deliveryman said. "Can I see your Global ID card, please?"

"No problem," said Willy, pulling the card from his pocket. The World Post man swiped it through a small box he carried and the information matched. "It's you, all right." He handed Willy some papers. "If you'll just fill in the spaces marked I'll be on my way."

Willy watched as the driver returned to his truck, then wheeled himself back into the house where he was surprised to see Thorold sitting at the computer trying to access the CD.

"Getting anywhere, Agent Stone?" he asked.

"Nope," admitted Thorold. "Same thing every time: 'Password required.'"

He watched as Willy tore the wrapping off the package and opened it, revealing a streamlined version of the high-tech glasses they had been wearing—small, lightweight, and ultrasophisticated. A tiny radio transceiver was built into one earpiece. The antenna integrated into the frame of the lenses. The contact points at the bridge of the nose and the forehead were skin sensors to interact with the brain. Willy put on his pair. The fit was snug and they were much better designed than his prototype and seemed to shape themselves to his forehead.

"See anything?" Thorold asked.

"Nothing," he replied. "These are the real ones, though. They'll be activated when the O.N.E. mainframe transmits its signal at noon on the Day of Wonders. That's when the whole world will see whatever's on that CD of yours."

"That's why I need to find out what's on that CD before the Day of Wonders," explained Thorold. "If it's got anything to do with Len then it's got to be stopped."

Willy shrugged. "So far it's your word against O.N.E.

I've seen their report on you and I've heard you out. The rest . . . I don't know."

"I'll tell you this," replied Thorold. "No matter what's on this disc, it's not going to be a walk on the beach."

Chapter

Anna Davis lay on her side, her wrists still bound behind her back and to the frame of the chair. She had been knocked over, landing painfully on her shoulder, the side of her head striking the concrete. Her throat was parched, there was a ringing in her ears, and one eye was swollen shut. She could no longer speak, but it did not matter. Len Parker knew there was nothing more she was going to say.

Anna knew that her husband had slipped Agent Stone the CD because he had sensed he was a man he could trust.

But had Thorold Stone joined the Christians? Somehow she doubted it. He was still too angry, too confused. But she also knew that he would need to find out what was on the CD, to evaluate it for himself. If he was able to learn the secret, maybe he would go against his training and loyalty oath to deliver it to the others. They would know how to use it. But all this was just speculation, the hopes of a desperate woman.

"Overlord Parker. Please meet Agent Dempsey at your office!" came a sudden announcement over the loudspeaker.

Parker looked down with contempt at the semiconscious woman on the floor then straightened his necktie, rolled down his shirtsleeves, and left the interrogation room, leaving her lying on the floor.

"Overlord Parker," said the nervous Agent Dempsey, hurrying down the hall to meet him.

"What is it?" demanded Parker. He was still furious with the agent over the botched warehouse operation.

"Sir," he reported, "the security system has been triggered on the Day of Wonders. Someone has tried to hack in."

"What's the back trace?" asked Parker. "The only people who have access are the design staff." Was there another traitor in their midst? Anna Davis was bad enough. This could be worse.

"The trace leads us to the home of one of our computer engineers, sir," the agent continued, "a William Holmes, designer of the security system and password-encoding protocol."

"We've patched Holmes through to a secure cell phone, Overlord Parker," said another agent, who had just joined them. "He says it's urgent that he talk with you."

Parker grabbed the telephone. "Parker here. What's going on, Holmes?"

"Some lunatic named Stone busted in here about an hour ago," said Willy over the phone. "He forced me to hack into the Day of Wonders database, but I deliberately gave the wrong password to prevent full entry."

"Is Stone still there?" asked Parker.

"I wouldn't be calling if he was," the scientist replied.

"When I told him I was setting off an alarm, he fled, but I did manage to plant a microchip on him before he took off. You should have no trouble following the Hater."

"Nice work, Holmes," Parker said. "Stay right there. We'll send some men down right away." He turned off the telephone.

"Get over there and take a scanner," he ordered the second agent. "Kill them both."

"Both, sir?" the agent stammered.

"You heard me," snapped Parker. "We can't have loose ends like that before the Messiah's big day."

"Do you want me to go with him, sir?" asked Dempsey as the agent hurried off.

"Don't you think you've done enough?" sneered Parker. "You had him in your hands and you let him go. Now he's a real threat to the Day of Wonders."

"But, sir," protested Dempsey. "You were the one who shot at him. You . . ." He stopped and swallowed hard.

Parker's voice became very soft, his eyes burning. "That kind of talk can get you killed, Dempsey. I don't need you. One Nation Earth doesn't need you. The Messiah doesn't need you. So what do you think that means?"

"That I'm fired?" Dempsey whispered, terrified.

"Too much paperwork," replied Parker, taking out a gun and shooting Dempsey in the head.

⁂

"That's all I can do," said Willy, "buy you a little time."

"Do you think they believed you?" asked Thorold.

Willy shrugged. "We knew the risks when we hacked into the security system at O.N.E. and jumped the password files. They were vulnerable to hacking, but they had an alarm system. It's like breaking into a house with a security system. You can get in, though once you're there, the alarm is ringing and the police are on the way. They're sending someone over, but I think he has to come all the way from headquarters, so we've got to move fast."

"What do you mean 'we'?"

"Look, Stone," replied Willy. "These guys want to avoid loose ends. Who's going to care if a guy in a wheelchair up and disappears? Like it or not, you've got yourself a partner. It's the only way I can stay alive."

"Then let's roll, Willy," said Thorold with a smile.

Taking the CD, a player, and some other equipment, Willy packed a case and began moving toward the door. "Let's go," he said. "This is going to be quite an adventure."

છ

Night had settled on the city, but in the basement of O.N.E. headquarters, harsh lights burned twenty-four hours a day, keeping the prisoners awake and disoriented.

"How long has Overlord Parker had the Davis woman in the interrogation cell?" asked Agent Phillips, the third-shift replacement who had arrived early and was trying to determine what he faced that night.

"Most of the day," replied another guard as he prepared to sign out.

"She must be important," Phillips mused. "This is not the type of case he normally handles himself."

"Something to do with a Day of Wonders CD," the other explained. "She used to work in the planning department. From what I've been hearing, he feels personally betrayed. And from the sound of her screams, I don't think Overlord Parker sees it as a minor offense."

Agent Phillips peered into the interrogation room where Anna Davis was leaning against the far wall, barely able to stand erect, her wrists still tied behind her back, her head hanging, and both eyes swollen. The chair had been moved to a far corner of the room and Len Parker hovered over her, all pretense of civility gone. His face was covered with sweat, his shirt was disheveled, his necktie askew. "What are you hanging on to, Christian?" he shouted. "Don't you see, you've lost? God has lost! We've destroyed His people. After the Day of Wonders, you and every other Hater will be dead or converted. The battle will be over— the war lost. There will be no Christian left alive, no one to celebrate the fairy tale of Jesus. It will be a new era, one in which we will rule with absolute authority. Your God will have no reason to return without anyone to welcome Him. His prophecy has failed. But you can save your life, Christian. Renounce Jesus Christ and live. Renounce Christ! There is no reason for you to have to endure any more pain." As if to emphasize his point, he slapped her hard across the face. Her head jerked and she slid to the floor whimpering as she collapsed in a heap.

"You can't escape me," Parker continued. "There is no power in His name. So what's your decision, Hater? I'm running out of patience, and you're running out of time."

Anna Davis raised her head slowly, as if called by a voice only she could hear. She painfully shifted her body, looking past Parker at something on the ceiling.

"Renounce him!" Parker screamed.

A peaceful smile grew on Anna Davis's swollen lips. "I can see Him," she said, her voice a hoarse whisper. "I can see Jesus standing at the Father's right hand."

"You're delusional!" Len Parker shouted, raising his own eyes to where she was looking. His mouth opened and he stared in horror, and when he finally could speak again, his voice was deep, the sound coming not from his vocal cords but from somewhere in the darkest depths of his soul. Barely conscious, Anna realized she was hearing a voice of "legion," the demonic presence mentioned in the Bible by Luke. She sensed the fear within the heart of her tormentor as she remembered the words: "What have we do to with thee, Jesus, thou Son of God? Art thou come hither to torment us before the time?"

Then shaking himself as if to break the spell, Parker raised his hand to strike Anna again.

Chapter 17

"HOW LONG DO YOU THINK they'll follow the blind alley I sent them down?" asked Willy, sitting in Thorold's car. His O.N.E. scanner was plugged into the lighter socket, and they were listening to calls being dispatched to tactical units.

"Five minutes. Five hours." Thorold shrugged. "It really doesn't matter, Willy. We have to assume that they'll throw a net over this city that's so tight no one will escape. Right now we're probably the two most wanted men in the world." He drove aimlessly, trying to blend with traffic, but knowing that the later the day became, with fewer people on the road, it would be harder to hide. They needed shelter, a place to plan their next move.

"I've got to have a computer to do anything," Willie explained to him. "I took the special peripherals, but I need something bigger and faster than your notebook. That means we're going to have to join the Haters."

"The Haters are locked away in that hellhole in the basement of the O.N.E. building," Thorold explained. "Assuming we could get in, we'd never get out alive."

"I'm talking about the ones that are still free," responded Willy.

"And just how are we supposed to find them?" Thorold demanded. "I'm an agent of O.N.E. assigned to round up Haters and even I don't know where to look. Besides, what makes you think we'd be welcomed by them? They may not be angry with the world the way Parker wants us to believe, but if I were them, I'd want nothing to do with either of us."

"I think we'll find ourselves most welcome," said Willy.

"Why?" queried Thorold. "Because you're wearing a white hat."

⋈

Agent Spencer moved cautiously through the wooded area a few blocks from the house of Willy Holmes. He was carrying a shotgun and a sidearm, both ready in case he spotted his targets.

Thorold Stone had already escaped from what should have been certain death. And Willy Holmes had received enough training to be deadly if armed. He needed to stay alert.

"Is Stone still backtracking?" he asked, looking down at the tracking monitor carried by Agent Walker, who had also been assigned to the case. Walker watched an LCD screen with a grid of city streets and a small blip moving in a seemingly random pattern. He changed the control to give him a magnified area to study and the screen indicated they were within one hundred yards of their quarry.

Moving forward, Walker drew his gun, positioning himself to keep Stone and Holmes off guard. Walker and Spencer were trained to back each other up, and procedures called for two or more O.N.E. agents to be involved in any takedown.

Spencer pressed the broadcast button on the tactical radio unit attached to his belt, activating the microphone clipped to his lapel. "We've got him on the monitor, Mr. Parker," Spencer whispered.

There was a pause while he listened, then replied, "No, sir. We don't have them in line of sight just yet. This is a wooded area, but the tracking unit is giving us excellent directions. No, sir, we won't lose them. They're backtracking to keep us off track, but from the grid map, we can follow every move." He listened for another moment, then signed off.

అఫ

With each new direction Willy gave Thorold, the car moved closer to the center of the city, where surveillance was likely to be more intense. "What do you think you're doing?" Thorold demanded. "You're taking us back toward WNN."

"We're going to visit some Haters," Willy explained.

"In the heart of Macalousso's media headquarters?" Thorold said skeptically. "Is this a setup, Willy?"

"Whether you believe me or not, I happen to know some Haters," the scientist explained. "They're located not far from here. I know for a fact that they've been using a hideout here for a few months."

"Assuming you're right, what makes you think they'll let us in?" asked Thorold. "From what we've been hearing on the dispatch tonight, they'll most likely shoot us and dump our bodies in the river. Why should any Hater risk his life for us?"

Willy looked down, saying nothing. "One of them is my sister," Willy whispered at last.

"Say that again?" said the startled Thorold.

"My sister. One of them is my sister," repeated Willy. "Why do you think I listened when you told me the Haters were being set up? I visit her whenever I think it's safe. I know I told you earlier that I had lost her, but I didn't know whether I could trust you." He pointed. "Right up there. Pull over in front of that green house." When the car stopped, Willy opened the door and whistled, staring into the darkness nervously when there was no response. Just his dog, Elvis, came bounding to the door. "Up!" said Willy, and the dog jumped happily onto his lap. He turned to Thorold and explained, "We have a friend who lives here. Elvis and me go visiting once in a while. It was so close, I knew he'd come here to wait for me." Willy took the dog's collar in his hand and carefully examined it. "It looks like someone found the tracking chip," he remarked.

As he petted Elvis, the voice of a dispatcher came on the radio. "Attention all units, investigators have located Agent Stone's microchip laced on another party as a diversion. The entire downtown core has been sealed. Orders remain unchanged for both Agent Stone and William Holmes. Both men are to be considered armed and dangerous and are to be shot on sight."

"Cool," said Willy as Thorold eased the car back in traffic. "Somebody thinks I'm dangerous. This is more exciting than any gunfight."

✢

John Goss was sitting at a large table, pondering a blue print unfolded in front of him that detailed the organization of the Day of Wonders. A schedule for virtual reality goggles to go to every citizen of the planet made clear the enormity of the Day of Wonders. Every man, woman, and child in the world was being equipped with the viewing device with broadcast units and transponders erected on tall buildings, in desert regions, rain forests, and in the polar caps. Wherever there were people, the deliveries were under way and a method for broadcasting the activator signals was in place.

Even the manufacture of the goggles was impressive. Regional factories had been established worldwide, in South Africa, Australia, China, and Germany, each producing a different part for the viewing devices including prisms. Radio receivers and more than sixty other parts were produced in six hundred regional factories in three shifts running seven days a week. No one who worked in a manufacturing plant had any contact with their counterparts in an assembly plant. And no one had more than one-sixtieth of the knowledge needed to learn the viewing devices.

The Day of Wonders was an undertaking unlike any other in history. That one person, even one with the powers of Macalousso, could plan, mount, and execute the manufacture and distribution of the goggles was almost beyond comprehension. It was only the fact that he and the others remained in hiding that gave Goss any hope. To be able to mount an event as elaborate as the Day of Wonders yet not be able to ferret out rebel Christians showed a real vulnerability. John Goss looked upon Franco Macalousso as his mortal enemy, as wicked as Hitler or Stalin, the embodiment of evil, but if he couldn't find their hideout maybe he could be stopped somehow, some way.

It was reasoning that frustrated Helen Hannah. "You've got to read the book," she kept telling him. "Franco Macalousso is the Antichrist, the fulfillment of prophecy. You call him your 'mortal enemy,' but he's much more than that. The Bible says the Antichrist is going to triumph. Many Christians will die by his hand, just as they are doing now. Many people will take on the mark of the Beast. Even those who once were our friends and neighbors, coworkers we thought we knew, they'll all worship the image of the Beast. And those of us who refuse will be killed. The time of the Antichrist has come just as it was foretold, and none of us can do anything about it."

"And where does the Day of Wonders fit in?" John asked.

"I don't know," Helen admitted. "I just haven't found anything in my studies that fits it into prophecy. That must mean the Day of Wonders is something God wants us to learn the truth about and expose. We've been safe here so far only because of the Lord's presence. We've got to preserve the knowledge of Jesus Christ, and I'm convinced that so long as we walk the path with Jesus, we have nothing to fear."

"And I think we've avoided capture because we picked a good place and we've been very lucky," countered John

Goss. "I've been reading Revelation like you asked me to, Helen, and other parts of the New Testament, too. I want to believe. I want to have your faith. But if I start thinking all this is inevitable, then what's the use? Macalousso is an evil man, maybe the most evil the world has ever seen. Maybe he is the Antichrist, but if we can frustrate his plans for this Day of Wonders, maybe others will see him as a fraud."

The argument always ended the same way, as Helen sighed with exasperation, gave him a hug, and handed him more books and tapes, whatever she thought would get him to truly consider the truth of the Antichrist.

Chapter

Now, with the Day of Wonders fast approaching, John Goss turned to her and asked, "Any word from Ronny?"

"Not yet," said Helen. "We know he's cleared the background check and that no one has connected him with us, thank God. He's now officially on Len Parker's security staff, which will give him the direct access to whatever was on that CD. How about you?" Helen asked. "Anything yet?"

"I'm still trying to figure out this goggle stuff," John admitted. "I keep wondering what they could possibly have to do with the Day of Wonders. But the only way we're going to get answers is to break into the O.N.E. computer system, and that's impossible."

The two talked, unaware that Willy had just rolled into the room. "I can get into the computer," said Willy quietly.

"Willy! Oh, thank God, you're alive!" cried Helen, rushing over to hug her brother. "We heard that you were kidnapped by a renegade O.N.E. agent."

Helen stopped staring at the man who entered moments after Willy as John drew a pistol from his pocket.

"Put that gun away, John," said Willy. "Thorold's okay. Give him a break."

"He's a cop, Willy," said John, still pointing the weapon. "An O.N.E. special agent. I heard on the news—"

"—that he's the one who kidnapped me," interrupted Willy. "But Thorold Stone isn't who they claim. He knows too much and now O.N.E. is after him, too."

Walking over to Goss, Helen took the weapon from him. Putting the safety on, she tucked the small gun back in his shirt pocket.

"Thanks," said a relieved Thorold. "I never thought I'd be beholden to Helen Hannah, the world's most wanted woman." Turning to Willy, he added, "You really should have told me, Willy. When you said your sister had been in television news, I never imagined she was one of the most respected people in the business."

"Would you have told me if the situation was reversed?" asked Willy. "Until I knew I could trust you, there was no way I was going to tell you everything."

"At least introduce us," interjected Helen. "All I know is that you're all over the news. Apparently people in high places don't like you very much. And these days, I have to say I admire that quality in a man."

"Helen," said Willy, "this is Thorold Stone. Thorold, I think you know my sister."

∽

At least the computer equipment was state of the art, which was the one advantage to having a sister who once worked for the world's largest television broadcast system. Still, it had taken Willy almost three hours to rewire the computers and install the special hardware he had brought with him from his lab.

Especially dangerous was trying to find ways to avoid traces when he hacked into the O.N.E. system. He wired in a cellular phone unit, then altered a line to move the feed around the country. It wouldn't prevent a trace, but it would confuse the O.N.E. system, taking extra time to locate the hacking source. But Willy dared not think about time or anything else that might distract him, which was why he was startled to hear the voice of Cindy Bolton behind him saying, "If you guys are hungry, there's some leftover salad in the fridge."

Willy turned and saw the blind woman Helen had mentioned, her beauty shining through despite the dark glasses she wore. "Salad? That's all you've got?" he teased. "I've worked hard to get to the top of the food chain and I didn't do it by eating vegetables."

"Well that explains a lot. Vegetables are brain food," teased Cindy right back.

Taking a break from his work, Willy wheeled over to where Cindy was standing and, looking into her eyes, asked, "Where have you been all my life?"

Helen and John laughed, relaxing a bit as they realized that nothing more could be done until Willy finished assembling the hardware and could go to work on the computer. As he worked intently, Cindy sat by his side, talking softly and occasionally reaching over to touch his shoulder.

John Goss returned to his schematics and charts, even

knowing in his heart that Willy's skills were their only hope of success. Yet, it was comforting to him to feel he was contributing with his efforts.

Helen sat with Thorold, drinking coffee and wrapped up in a deep discussion. "Thorold Stone, I'm surprised at you," Helen was saying. "You actually think that Franco Macalousso's some kind of space alien? This is real life, not some science fiction fantasy. The Bible has been warning us about this for centuries, but those of us who have been left behind were too foolish to heed the Word."

"I went to church a few times with Wendy and the kids," said Thorold. "I never heard about anything like this."

"You have to read the Bible," she explained, picking up the book and thumbing through it. "This is history. This is prophecy. This is God speaking to us through the ages. You know all the things we've seen, the so-called miracles? Here in the twenty-fourth chapter of Matthew it says, 'For there shall arise false Christs, and false prophets, and shall show great signs and wonders; insomuch that, if it were possible, they shall deceive the very elect.' And in the second chapter of Second Thessalonians, it refers to the Antichrist: 'Even him, whose coming is after the working of Satan with all power and signs and lying wonders, and with all deceivableness.' Does that sound familiar? God doesn't use aliens to fulfill Bible prophecy. We're seeing what the writer of Revelation revealed in chapter 13 when he wrote, 'And I beheld another beast coming up out of the earth; and he had two horns like a lamb, and he spoke as a dragon. And he exerciseth all the power of the first beast before him, and causeth the earth and them which dwell therein to worship the first beast, whose deadly wound was healed. And he doeth great wonders, so that he maketh fire come down from heaven on the earth in the sight of men, and deceiveth them that dwell on the earth by the means of those miracles which he had power to do in the sight of the beast.' Thorold, the first beast is Macalousso, the Antichrist. The other beast is the false prophet."

"Len Parker?" asked Thorold. He had been listening intently, uncertain of what he believed yet, but seriously considering what Helen had to say.

"I don't know," she admitted. "Maybe. What matters is that we are living in the days that were foretold for those of us who failed to be raptured like Wendy and your daughters."

"I understand what you're telling me, but I'm trained to deal in facts," protested Thorold.

"These are facts," she insisted. "Why do you think it's illegal to have a Bible, that people who dare to proclaim the Word of God are 'reeducated,' tortured, and killed? He has targeted only those who have come to know the Word of Christ."

Thorold frowned. "Helen, I saw Len Parker go through a wall. He shot me, then turned and walked out of the room and the only thing there was solid brick. That's not a power any earthly man has."

"You experienced the parlor tricks of the Beast," she insisted. "There is only one truth and that's God's truth. These people aren't aliens trying to re-create prophecy. God's hand is in this. People like Len Parker have made choices, horrible choices. They may have dramatic powers, but at the cost of their immortal souls. Stop trying to analyze everything based on your old beliefs. Think about what I just read to you. What we're all experiencing has been foretold and God has been working in your life, too."

"God? My life?" he replied bitterly. "Do you mean Wendy and the kids?"

"I'm not talking about the Rapture," she countered. "That was something they earned, a reward for recognizing what the rest of us didn't understand. No, Thorold, I'm talking about what brought you to our door. You don't think it was chance. You're here because God has a plan for you."

"Not me," said Thorold, genuinely surprised by the idea. "I didn't buy the idea when my wife was selling it, and I'm sure not going to buy it from you." He was becoming annoyed, though whether it was with Helen or with himself he wasn't sure. It made him uneasy to think he might be an important player in all this. "Helen," he continued, "my mom believed in God with all her heart when I was a little kid. Then she got cancer. She'd pray to God for peace, but all I could see on her face were pain and anguish. When she got too weak to pray, I prayed for her. I made all sorts of deals with Him. I promised to clean my room. I promised to be a good boy. I had always been taught that children were important to Jesus, that if we asked without being selfish, God would grant us what we asked. Then Mom died. At first I refused to believe what was happening. Then we went to the funeral home. When no one was looking, I touched her, trying to get her to wake up. That's when I realized she wasn't my mother anymore, but just an empty body. That night I went into my room and told God I hated Him for taking a good woman like my mother."

There were tears in his eyes, and his voice was soft and intense. Looking past Helen, past the physical barriers of the room, he was seeing the past again, remembering his mother and the feelings of losing her.

Helen reached over and touched his hand, and he gripped it tightly. "I couldn't understand how God could take my mother away from me like that," he continued. "I tried for a long time to answer that question, but I couldn't. That's why I think the answer is simpler than you might want to hear."

"Tell me, Thorold," said Helen softly. "I lost both of my parents when I was young. My grandmother raised Willy and me. I understand more than you think. There are situations that don't have the outcome we desire. Yet in God's way, they work out for the best. That's why I know you're making a mistake by doubting God. You and my brother."

Willy looked up from the computer and said, "Let me ask you something, Helen. If a man speaks in the forest and there's no woman there to hear him, is he still wrong?"

Thorold laughed at the joke; Helen smiled and shook her head. "All right, you guys. So we all know where we disagree. Now get back to work, Willy." Turning to Thorold, she added, "Let's keep talking and see where we do agree."

"Okay," said Thorold, feeling peace now in the presence of this woman. As far as he was concerned, it was pure luck that they were still alive. If Helen had other ideas, he could at least hear her out.

"Thorold, I've been in broadcasting more years than I

want to admit," Helen continued. "I'm as cynical as you are, maybe more. And I lost the most important person in my life in the Rapture. But there is no question in my mind that Bible prophecy is being fulfilled exactly as written. Just remember, the book was written long before anyone heard of Franco Macalousso, or the Church of One Nation Earth. This is the story of our past and the foretelling of our future. The New World Order has as one of its primary goals the creation of a one-world church. There would be no chance for dissent, no way for scholars to disagree. The Word of God has been subverted in the name of unity. People have been trying to achieve this one-world church for over 150 years. Now it's becoming institutionalized as the United Religious Organization."

"Helen, Thorold, John, I'm ready!" shouted Willy, interrupting his sister as they all hurried over to the computer screen.

"There's still one line encrypted," Willy explained, "but it won't stop me from running the program. I'll keep trying to crack it, but at least now we can take this baby for a test drive."

Clicking the mouse, Willy ran the program with no error message. Moving to a second computer interlinked with the first, he called up the words "Select Virtual World," the same message that was on the screen at Willy's home when he had taken Thorold for a virtual walk on the beach. But now there was only one option to choose, "Day of Wonders."

"You're into the Day of Wonders disc?" asked Helen. Her brother said nothing as he activated the program, sat back in his chair, and put on the goggles. A voice was saying, "Welcome to the Day of Wonders."

Chapter

THE VIRTUAL WORLD WAS OVERWHELMINGLY, blindingly white, with no sense of up or down, no horizon or shadow to guide him.

Willy squinted and shielded his eyes, trying to adjust to the intensity, and for several moments stood where he was before he began to walk in what he hoped was a straight line, trying to see something, anything. He called out, trying to hear if anyone else occupied his virtual world, but there was no sound, and no echo. "This is the Day of Wonders?" Willy said, as much to himself as to the others. "What's the big deal?" He removed the goggles.

"So what was it?" asked Thorold.

"Nothing," said Willy dejectedly.

"What do you mean, 'nothing'?" demanded Thorold. "Could you walk? Talk? Was it like the beach?"

"It was nothing, a white nothing," Willy insisted. "Picture the opposite of everything. Zero. Zilch. Other than the fact that I could stand and walk, there's nothing to this program at all."

"You're wrong, Willy," said Thorold. "There's something on that disc. There must be. As good as you are, you missed it."

Willy frowned. "I told you what happened," he said, annoyed.

"And I believe you," Thorold assured him, "but I'm a trained investigator. I know how to interpret seemingly unrelated facts, to find patterns. Len Parker is trying to kill us because we have this CD. Why?"

Willy sighed, pulled the goggles back over his eyes, tapped on the keyboard, then began moving his upper body first one way and then another, obviously exploring the white nothing he had just left.

Helen took Thorold's hand and led him back to the table where they had been talking. "We're going to finish our discussion while Willy works, Thorold," she told him.

"You're forgetting one thing, Helen," he reminded her. "I don't believe in God."

"But God believes in you," she replied, "and He's still God, whether you believe in Him or not."

"Well, if He's for real, why doesn't He just show Himself?" Thorold asked. We've got Satan or the Antichrist down here disguised as Franco Macalousso. Why doesn't He just show Himself, blast Macalousso with a lightning bolt, and let us get on with our lives?"

"I hear that question a lot from unbelievers," she responded. "In fact, I used to ask it myself."

"Helen, your parents were killed," he said, taking her hand again. "Your grandmother was taken from you. You've lost your job. You're a fugitive with a price on your head. Where is God in the midst of this hell?"

"He's all around us," she replied with certainty.

"I know that one," Thorold protested. "They used to throw it at us in Sunday school. About how He's present in the birds that fly, the grass that grows, the flowers that bloom. We even had songs about it, but I don't remember them anymore. The point is, if there's a God, I should be able to put Him to the test. I mean, I'm sitting with some of the last believers left alive on the earth. He needs to keep your faith strong, right?"

"We need to keep *our* faith strong, Thorold," she replied. "God's always with us. We just don't always reach out to Him."

Thorold took a water glass and moved it to the center of the table. "If God wants to show me His presence, have Him knock over that water glass."

"If He did that, you wouldn't need much in the way of faith, would you?" asked Helen.

"But if it's faith, where's the proof?" demanded Thorold.

"Oh, it's not all faith, Thorold," Helen countered. "God says all you need is faith the size of a mustard seed and He'll do the rest."

"I've heard that one, too. But that's not proof."

"No proof is enough if your heart's not ready," she responded softly, looking deeply into his eyes. "Let's get personal," she continued. "I don't know what you've experienced in your life that would have proved that God was real. But remember the day when the Christians disappeared? We didn't know what to call it then because we didn't know about the Rapture, but you know your wife and children were good people, believers, with faith at least the size of that mustard seed."

"I'd rather not talk about that, Helen," he objected.

"All of us suffered losses that day," she insisted. "There were Christians in all our lives, people we knew and loved. And they knew God in their hearts in ways the rest of us never did. God took the Christians as He promised, but His love remains. He stayed with us, trying to lead us to His truth, and with time, He succeeded. We found Bibles when we were ready to finally listen. We found tapes and books left behind by the Christians who were raptured. We read the Word, we listened to Christian leaders whose words remained even after they were gone. And gradually, one by one, we opened our hearts to the Lord."

"That's how you see it," contended Thorold.

"That's how Franco Macalousso sees it," Helen insisted. "Who is the enemy in the eyes of Macalousso? Christians. Who is he trying to kill? Christians. This so-called Messiah claims to have taken all the people who were evil, the ones he calls the Haters. But if Franco Macalousso is an alien, and if he made every one of his enemies disappear, then why can't he do that again? A power like that doesn't need law enforcement officers. The truth is that Macalousso is Satan, the Antichrist, and his powers, though impressive, are as nothing compared with those who speak the name of Jesus. God is with us. His love protects us and keeps us safe while we keep His word alive.

Macalousso fears anyone having the Word or even those books, tapes, and literature that were left behind after the Rapture."

Thorold was deeply moved by Helen's words yet at the same time, he still was not ready to believe. He sat there looking at the drinking glass, at Helen, and then at the ceiling. "Come on, God!" he shouted. "Knock it over right now and I'll believe in You! You couldn't save my mother when I was a little boy, but maybe You can knock over one little glass of water. Helen said you can do anything and all I'm asking is for You to knock over this glass."

Helen's eyes filled with tears, her heart heavy. "Forgive him, Lord, he knows not what he is doing," she whispered.

"Looks like God's not up to the challenge," Thorold said with a cynicism that belied the catch in his voice as he fought to hide the emotions overwhelming him. "I guess Macalousso's the only one doing miracles these days."

Thorold felt like a bully, one who had deliberately used words to hurt Helen, and he was not proud of himself. Not knowing what to say or do, he announced, "This is ludicrous. I need some fresh air," and stood up abruptly, sending the glass of water flying, its water spraying across the table, the glass itself spinning to a stop.

Thorold stared at it, his emotions at their limit, then turned and left the building without another word, walking into an empty field behind the hideout. It was a clear night, the stars like a quilt that could cover the earth with its warmth. Tears streamed down his face as he stared at the vastness. "I'm not looking for God!" he whispered, the words coming haltingly. "I'm just trying to find my family . . ."

༶

Len Parker sat in his office behind a locked door, his computer on a secure link to the personnel files. On the screen was the complete file on Thorold Stone, his wife, and his children, photographs, DNA charts, and copies of dental X-rays. The man's whole history was before him, but what he did not have was Stone himself, and he felt impotent without the man under lock and key. The powers that had come to him were like those of the ancient gods of Mt. Olympus. So why could he not find one special agent?

Chapter

CINDY BOLTON WAS A ROMANTIC, delighting in stories of medieval damsels and bold knights who adored the king's beautiful daughter, locked in a tower. In Cindy's mind, she was the maiden who wore gossamer garments flowing in the wind when the knight rescued her and carried her away on the back of his magnificent steed.

Cindy had listened to every talking book she could find on such romantic themes. Real romance had never been a part of her life, even though she had tried to be like others, to fit in, even when she was uncomfortable with the choices of the crowd. She had dated because her friends had dates, encouraging boys she should have discouraged because she hoped they found her desirable, not just a girl with a good figure who might be grateful for their attention.

Disillusioned, she retreated once more into the talking books that fueled her fantasies, not realizing that she had the type of face and figure that caused men to turn and stare when she walked down the street.

She understood the risk she was taking after the day of the Disappeared, when she had found audiotapes of the

Bible and sermons by ministers who had vanished with most of her church congregation. She listened out of curiosity at first, before realizing the speakers were making sense, as she heard the Bible come alive for her in ways she had never before thought possible. Cindy had avoided church her whole adult life, but now found herself drawn to this man called Jesus, a man who loved the outcasts most of all. And when she realized that Franco Macalousso was a false Messiah, she accepted the fact that becoming a Christian would mean she spent the rest of her life in greater isolation than she had ever known in blindness.

Now, after months of self-imposed exile in which her romantic fantasies were nothing but cruel jokes, she had at last found her knight in shining armor, a computer genius who rode a gleaming wheelchair. And rather than carrying her off to a kingdom far, far away, he had come to share her tower imprisonment.

Cindy knew that Willy's legs were withered, but she knew little else of how he looked. But it didn't matter. She had often been angry with God in the past, questioning how much He truly loved His people. But if God had brought her Willy, perhaps He really did care for His creatures.

She walked over to where Willy was working, massaging his neck as he took off his goggles and held out his hand to help her sit down. He stared into her glasses, as though she could see his smile, and he knew that she liked him, regardless of his physical limitations. Talking with her was like talking to someone he had known all his life, someone who shared his sense of humor, and the laughter that came from overcoming hardships. "Let me ask you something, Cindy," he said. "If blind people wear sunglasses, why don't deaf people wear earmuffs?"

Cindy laughed. "Let me ask you something, Willy. Do men in wheelchairs complain if you leave the seat up?"

He joined the laughter, slipping his hand from hers and reaching up to touch her face. Stroking her forehead, he ran his fingers down her jawline and she tilted her head against his hand as he touched her cheek. He reached up and carefully removed the glasses from her face, then put his hand under her chin, tilting her head so her eyes would catch more of the light, showing nothing but white.

"You're the most beautiful girl I've ever seen," he whispered. "Don't hide behind dark glasses."

Cindy took Willy's hand and held it tight against her face. "Do you know how long I've wanted to hear someone say that?" she asked.

Willy cleared his throat, suddenly uncomfortable with the intimacy. "So what made you decide to become a Christian?" he asked, wanting to change the subject.

"I think you're assuming more about me than you should," she replied. "To be honest, I'm not sure what I believe. My mom and dad made the church the focus of their life. I know now that's why they were raptured, but it was different for me. Some of the church members used to talk about my blindness as punishment for past sins. They said I must have done something wrong. There were days I wanted to scream at them, to tell them how wrong they were, yet in my heart I feared they were right. I felt like God was punishing me for a life I hadn't really lived. But when my parents vanished along with all of their church friends, I had nowhere to turn. Then John invited me to come with him. I guess you could say I'm sort of along for the ride." She paused. "But what about you, Willy? What do you believe?"

"The truth?" he said. "Despite my sister's faith, I still believe Franco Macalousso is exactly who he says he is, the Messiah. I also believe that the Day of Wonders program is the work of the most evil men I've ever known. They're not doing the Messiah's work and I doubt that the Messiah has any idea what is taking place in his name. I'm convinced it's up to us to find out what they're up to."

༄

He knew there was a risk in going out, walking the back roads behind the WNN headquarters, yet in spite of the risk Thorold felt safe.

He was a police officer, trained to think like a police officer, which meant looking at situations logically. He knew that a man on the run could certainly flee quickly, his every thought on avoiding detection and capture.

To walk these back roads in a quiet park setting was not a move any fugitive would take; to appear lost in thought and unconcerned if a car approached was not fugitive behavior. That's what he would have told himself if he was in the patrol car looking for a wanted man. That's what Smitty would have done.

Thorold sat by the rocks of the quiet stream, staring at the photo of Wendy and the kids in the moonlight. It was the kind of place he and Wendy had gone when dating, holding each other as they planned their future, a peaceful place with a sense of safety and serenity. He needed to think, to put what was happening in perspective. Thorold picked up a stone and tossed it into the water, watching the moonlit reflection break into shimmering ripples, then threw another, and another. Suddenly a stone skipped across the surface of the stream from behind him. Startled, Thorold turned to see Helen.

"You've got to use flat ones if you want them to skip," she said with a smile. "And you've got to throw them with a sidearm motion. Boys are so busy trying to get distance, they never learn to finesse the rock." Gesturing toward the rock on which he had been sitting, she asked, "Room for one more?"

Thorold nodded and Helen sat down next to him. In silence, Thorold stared across the water, then spoke in a soft voice. "They say you have to lose something before you can appreciate just how much it meant? Right now, I'd give anything just to have my girls wake me up from a nap on the couch by fighting over the TV remote. Can you imagine? How I used to long for a little peace and quiet. Now I just wish I had a chance to see them once more, to hold them in my arms."

Helen did not answer, but simply sat watching the water, her arms around her knees. "I never had a family of my own," she said at last. "I was always too busy, too caught up in my career. I told myself I was a modern woman who valued success and achievement and money, the important things in life. Can you believe that?" She turned to him.

"Tell me, Thorold, if you could see your kids right now, what would you tell them?"

"That I love them," he said, his voice choking with emotion. "That I've always loved them and I always will. A part of me was torn away forever and I would give anything to know they were safe and at peace."

"Sounds to me like you've pretty well figured out what's important in life," said Helen. She was smiling, but her words were in earnest.

"What do you mean?" he asked.

"I'm talking about God," she replied. "Think about it, Thorold. Molly and Maggie were your creation with Wendy, just like we are all a part of God's creation. But it's more than that. When a child is born, it is the result of a man, a woman, and God all working together. God loves us because He shares in our creation. He died for His creation just like you would die for yours. You and He both agree on what is most important in life. You say you like to deal in logic," she said, turning to him. "Then do it! Do you really think you're being logical about what's happening in the world today? Do you think you're being logical now?"

"What are you saying?" he replied in frustration. "What's your point?"

"Think about Franco Macalousso," she challenged him. "Do you think he knows what Len Parker and the others are doing in his name?"

"He doesn't know everything," said Thorold. "If he did, you Haters wouldn't have survived so long on the run. He's trying to do to Christians what Hitler did with the Jews—

depersonalize them, lump them together and call them evil and unclean. Hitler was the embodiment of evil and so is Franco Macalousso."

"But, think about what he's saying," urged Helen. "He claims to be our creator, but his message isn't about love at all. It's about power and selfishness. About each person getting whatever they want regardless of the cost. Macalousso is encouraging them to destroy anyone whose personal desires interfere with their own. It's the survival of the greediest, the most self-centered. Can you imagine if your daughters were with you and you had to teach them about life? Can you imagine yourself sitting down and telling your children that in the name of success, they should eliminate anyone who stands in the way of their dreams?"

Thorold stared at her. What she was saying made sense, terrifying sense.

"It's the same lie the serpent used on Eve in the Garden of Eden," Helen continued. "He told her to eat the fruit— that it wouldn't hurt her, that God was just afraid that if she ate it, she'd be just like Him."

"I know that story; I guess every kid learns it," he said. "But as an adult, I see something else. I see this God of yours just sitting there, powerless."

"He's not just sitting there, Thorold," she countered. "Far from it. His love is so great, He can be with us and still let us stumble. When your own children were babies, you were with them all the time. You guided and nurtured them. But you had to let them find their own way, even if it meant they would stumble and fall. Your love was so great that you gave them the chance to grow on their own, hoping your guidance and the knowledge they gained from making mistakes would be enough. Franco Macalousso's a parlor magician on a grand scale, but he was just fulfilling God's plan. God doesn't need thought police to kill anyone who disagrees with Him. God doesn't need to dominate the media to show us how wonderful He is. God doesn't want us to believe out of fear. After all, Jesus appealed to the dead after His crucifixion, so certainly even the worst of us can repent, and if we are sincere, we can join our Father in heaven. God doesn't want to win you with cheap tricks and flattery. He wants you to search your heart and ask yourself, 'Do I believe Him? Do I believe He loves me? Do I believe that He died for me and for my sins?"

She reached out and took Thorold's hand as he continued to stare across the water for a moment, then turned to her. She reminded him then of Mrs. Davis. He had been one of her tormentors, one of her persecutors, and yet there was no hint of animosity in her eyes.

"It's time for you to decide what you believe, Thorold Stone," she said and, releasing his hand, rose to her feet, quietly walking back toward the hideout as he stayed behind looking out across the moonlit water.

Chapter 21

SLEEP CAME TO JOHN, Helen, and the others in fits and starts, some sleeping during the day, some at night, and some only in snatches.

Willy should have been as exhausted as the rest, but the chance to talk with his sister kept him awake and alert. Sitting at a table drinking coffee, they argued as they had done after their grandmother disappeared and Helen had begun reading the Bible she had left behind.

Willy was a pragmatist, separating Franco Macalousso from his closest associates, convinced that Len Parker and the leadership staff of O.N.E. were corrupt and evil; exactly the opposite of the man he believed to be the Messiah. Still, Helen tried to reason with him even as Willy became increasingly frustrated with her.

"I don't want to hear about it!" Willy complained. "I know who Macalousso is and I don't believe—"

Willy stopped as at the door, a man in a O.N.E. security uniform appeared. "Storm troopers," he had once jokingly called such men. "Jackbooted storm troopers." Like everyone else, he had heard rumors of what these thugs did to Haters. And, like everyone else, he believed that the stories of tortures and executions were wildly exaggerated. But now that he was underground and on the run, he thought differently. He was a target of O.N.E., shortly to join the Haters in Len Parker's notorious interrogation cells.

"Thorold!" Willy shouted, bringing Thorold instantly awake. He dropped, rolled, and pulled out his gun, determined to kill as many as he could to protect the others.

Ron Wolfman, the man in uniform, instinctively drew his own weapon, aiming at Thorold while at the same moment, Helen threw herself between them shouting, "Stop! Both of you!"

Easing their fingers off the triggers, they were uncertain what was happening. Both still poised for action. "It's okay," Helen explained. "We're all on the same side here." She went over to Ronny and gave him a hug. Thorold slowly holstered his weapon, and only then did Ronny put away his gun.

"Thorold Stone, I want you to meet Ronny Wolfman," Helen said. "As you can see, Ronny has infiltrated Macalousso's forces."

Thorold nodded, relieved. "How do you do, Ronny?" he said, shaking hands.

"A lot better than Anna Davis," Ronny said sadly, turning to the others. "I had access to the monitoring equipment in the interrogation room and made a copy of the tape from the internal security camera." He frowned. "It's worse than we think. I doubt that St. Paul endured what some of these people have been put through. Anyway, you'll hear for yourself."

Ron crossed to a tape machine and pushed "Play" after inserting the tape. The voice of Len Parker filled the room. "God has lost! We've destroyed His people," he said. "After the Day of Wonders, you and every other Hater will be dead or converted. The battle will be over—the war lost . . . It will be a new era, one in which we will rule with absolute authority . . . You can save your life, Christian. Renounce Jesus Christ and live . . . There is no reason for you to have to endure any more pain."

There were sounds of a violent slap, a head striking the wall, a gasp, a scream, and another moan. As everyone cringed at the sounds, Ron's face paled and he turned off the machine. "I'm sorry," he whispered. "I wasn't there. I couldn't stop it."

Helen touched his shoulder. "It's not your fault, Ronny. No one blames you."

"You couldn't have stopped it even if you had been there," said Thorold quietly. "I shot Len Parker; I emptied my gun into him and nothing happened. Then he walked through a solid wall. The man has been given incredible powers."

"Mrs. Davis is still alive," Ronny informed them. "I just don't know if she wants to be."

"But at least we know more about the Day of Wonders," said Helen.

Thorold began pacing nervously. There was something more to all this, something they were missing. "It just doesn't make sense," he said at last. "What about the ones he vaporized? Is he planning to . . ."

"He didn't vaporize anyone, Thorold," interrupted Helen. "They were raptured. God called them home. Your family is in heaven. Your wife and daughters. You don't want to hear that, but truth is truth."

Suddenly there was a loud sound of static, and Len Parker's voice filled the room. "Hello, Special Agent Stone."

"It's the police monitor, Thorold," Willy told the startled agent. "I rigged it so we would hear any calls Parker made on his private frequency. I'm sure he knows we can monitor him."

Thorold's heart was racing as he listened to Parker's voice saying, "I know you're out there listening from somewhere, Stone," he said with contempt. "I thought you might be interested in some special guests visiting me here in my office."

There was a slight shift in the sound, one that only Willy caught. Something was not quite normal, but he could not tell just what.

"Please don't hurt us," said a woman's voice. "We don't know anything. I haven't seen him in months."

Willy looked at Thorold's pale face and realized the voice was Wendy. He had heard Thorold's story about the day of the disappearance and he had witnessed others disappear himself. But wherever they had gone, whatever happened to them, they weren't going to suddenly appear in the office of Overlord Len Parker.

"Wendy . . . ?" whispered Thorold.

The sound of a little girl in pain, her voice rising in a wail of agony, could be heard. Thorold's fists clenched, and his face was a mix of terror and hate.

"Mommy, why doesn't Daddy come and save us?" said the voice of his daughter, Maggie.

Parker's menacing voice was heard again. "Silence! Do you want to spend more time in the chamber?"

The voices quieted as the outlaws stood at the monitors, listening intently.

"Stone," said Parker. "You have one choice and one choice only, so you had better listen very carefully. I want you here at O.N.E. headquarters by 2:00 A.M., with the CD. Have you got that? Two A.M. If you refuse then your family will be the first ones to find out what the Day of Wonders is all about."

As Helen listened she knew in her heart that whatever Parker was doing to re-create their voices, he did not actually have Wendy and the children. They had been raptured, and were safe and at peace, where no evil could touch them.

This so-called Messiah was nothing but an impotent fraud who needed Parker to do his dirty work. He had to have the CD, and was threatened by a simple electronic device. If only Thorold could see the truth.

❧

Len Parker stood in his office, relishing the powers the Messiah had bestowed on him. His normally deep baritone transformed into a perfect imitation of Wendy's lilting soprano voice. "Please, don't hurt my daughters. They didn't do anything. Please, you . . ." He released the button, ending the broadcast.

⌘

Willy had returned to work trying to unravel the last pieces of the Day of Wonders CD, but there was a desperation to his actions now, as time was quickly growing short.

Thorold, meanwhile, was pacing like a caged animal. "I can't wait for Willy to crack this thing, Helen," he fumed. "You heard what Parker said. He's got Wendy and the kids. I've got no choice." Thorold paused, then turned angrily toward Helen. "So much for your heaven theory!" he spat.

"Please, Thorold, you've got to listen to me," she pleaded. "It's a trick."

"She's right," said Ronny. "If he had them, they would have been dead already."

"I know he's just using them to get me to go there," Thorold said angrily. "But I also know I don't have any choice."

Willy looked up from his work. "I think I may have a plan," he said. "The mainframe computer at O.N.E. is the hub for their entire system. Whatever we do to it will affect every other computer they use. If we could upload a virus to the main file server, it could theoretically infect every computer on their network."

"So what?" asked Ronny skeptically.

"Meaning that if it works, we can keep the sun from rising on the Day of Wonders."

"But what about that line of code?" Thorold asked. "Without it, all you saw was white. It must be the missing piece to whatever is going to happen. Have you been able to break it as yet?"

"I think I know how to crack it," Willy revealed. "However, I don't think that's the answer."

Thorold was startled. "But I thought you were counting on it," he said.

"Remember that seashell on the beach?" asked Willy

"I'll never forget it," said Thorold.

"Creating that single shell took almost four thousand lines of computer code," Willy explained. "So whatever their plan is for the Day of Wonders, it's not all on that disc."

"We've got to stop wasting time," insisted Thorold. "Whatever is or isn't on that disc isn't going to keep my family alive. I've got to go in there and get them."

"There's only one way to do that," said Willy. "I can get into the security files and have you authorized as a janitor."

Two hours later Helen Hannah returned from a variety store where she had bought a pair of overalls, a work shirt, and a baseball cap to create Thorold's janitor uniform. Outside their hideout she beat the clothing against the wall and the ground to make it just dirty enough to look authentic.

"Should I be carrying tools or something?" Thorold asked after changing into the clothes.

"No need," replied Ron. "There are stations throughout the building for cleaning and maintenance supplies. Just act natural, like you belong there."

"Are you sure you can find the VR lab once you're inside?" asked Helen.

Thorold nodded. "As long as the blueprints Willy pulled down are complete."

"They should be," Willy assured him. "I've marked the pathways from the different entrances so you can get to any place in the building and get out."

"What about the alarm systems?" asked Thorold.

"There are two systems," replied Willy. "The first is a monitoring alarm, with hidden cameras throughout the building. The guards are expected to check the monitors for authorized personnel and their locations."

"That won't be a problem," added Ronny. "Security's tight for the first two shifts, but the third shift is only pre-cleared personnel, so the interior alarm checks are usually ignored."

"And the second system?" asked Thorold.

"That can be trouble," admitted Willy. "Certain sections of the building have alarms that are separate from main security, such as the VR lab. Fortunately, these have been linked to the larger security system, which has deactivation points. I've marked them on the map."

"Then it should be a piece of cake," said Thorold.

"Not really," replied Willy. "There's only a limited time you can work before the system sets off a separate alarm. And there's a routine feedback to the monitor every few minutes. If someone's watching, they'll know it's not working. They should be lax on the third shift, but you never know. You won't have much time to get what you're after. I've created a secure channel on the radio I want you to carry. Just make certain you keep the transceiver under your shirt and slip the earpiece off before you go in. I'll keep the monitor up loud. Anytime you need me, just yell."

Thorold stared at Willy, suddenly realizing the enormity of his task. His next thought was of Wendy and his
children. He inhaled deeply, smiled, and said, "Let's do it."

Helen took his hand in both of hers, "Godspeed,
Thorold," she whispered.

⚬⚬

Len Parker didn't have time to worry about Thorold Stone.
There were only a few more hours until the Day of Wonders
was upon them and although the CD was still missing, the
security code seemed to have worked flawlessly. If he found
Thorold Stone he would torture him, slowly, painfully, until
he begged to have him end it all. And if he didn't . . . well,
in a few hours it would not matter anyway. But for now, it
was time to prepare. The Chosen One had been taken from
her holding cell. And the women were already performing
the ritual cleansing. Soon they would prepare the circle,
draw the sacred symbols, and then bind her within and drain
her life essence for the glorious ceremony.

Chapter 22

"YOU OKAY, WILLY?" asked Cindy, her hands on his shoulders as he sat perched over the computer equipment. On one monitor was the graphic of the CD with the security system of all but the final line of coding penetrated. His work had been flawless, and the mainframe system had not detected the breach. But there was still that final line of code.

"I don't know what else I can do." He sighed. "There has to be something in there." Willy typed rapidly on the keyboard as the image on the screen twisted and turned, spinning left and right, but ultimately stopping where it always had. "It's just one line of code. One simple line."

"Then why have they gone to all this trouble to keep you out?" she asked.

Willy leaned his head against Cindy's shoulder. She was right and he knew it. That last line was a key that would unlock the secrets and get the program activated. As much as he didn't want to admit it, that one line was the key component in the fate of the world. He looked down at his watch. "I'd better call Thorold," he said and rolled over to a broadcast unit where he accessed the security center's computer, using a split screen to run their system and crosschecking it against the clearance he had created for Thorold.

"I'm about three minutes out," reported Thorold as the speaker magnified the sounds of traffic as he drove into the city. "How are you doing back there?"

Willy scanned the computer screen, checking his work. "No problem," he replied. "I'm just making sure that you're supposed to be on duty tonight."

Willy found the name "David Nidd," an employee similar in age to Thorold and not working the shift. He quickly switched to Thorold's file, found the fingerprint for crossmatch identification, and stored it in the memory, replacing Nidd's fingerprint with Thorold's. The finger scan matched perfectly.

"Okay, your name is David Nidd and you're working the night shift," he told Thorold. The fingerprint scan is in place. Just remember your name." He paused. "And good luck, pal."

"Thanks," said Thorold. "I'm almost there. I'm going to stop the car long enough to turn off the transmitter and hide the receiver under my clothes. You sure about the fingerprint check?"

"Absolutely. It will register David Nidd," Willy answered him.

"I'm counting on you, buddy," said Stone, pulling the car to a stop.

"You are blessed to be part of this night," said one of the robed figures approaching the cell of a petite brunette who had just turned twenty-eight. Her name was Linda Gardner, a new Christian who had always maintained high moral standards despite her religious doubts. Her fiancé, also a new Christian, had been killed shortly after his arrest a few weeks earlier. She prayed nightly that they would be reunited in heaven.

The robes of the participants had monk's hoods, covering their heads and casting their faces in shadows. They spoke quietly of their delight in being present with one so honored, one chosen to pass over to the other side and know the joy of the world that the Messiah had promised.

Linda stood at the back of her cell, as if crouching in the corner might somehow save her from her fate. "Jesus loves you," she declared even now. "Why not open your hearts to Him? It's never too late."

"Do you realize the glory the Messiah has arranged for you?" spoke one of the figures. "Why do you persist in blasphemy? Where is this Jesus when you need Him? He's nothing but dust, rotted flesh two thousand years old, if He even lived at all."

"You have no idea, do you?" Linda retorted defiantly. "It is my turn to carry the cross for the love of our Father."

One of the hooded figures looked at the other and said, "Overlord Parker was right. There is a fire in her damnable heart. She is truly the one for tonight."

"I am not going with you," said Linda.

"Oh, but you will," replied one of the figures. "You have

been chosen. We must bathe and dress you to prepare for the ceremony."

Linda's heart was racing, her skin cold and clammy. "I am not going with you, you living demons from hell," she spat. "In Jesus' name, get out."

"No need to make this more difficult," said another robed figure. "We only wish to prepare you. It is our honor."

Dear Lord, if this is Your will for me, give me the strength to endure this, Linda prayed silently. *Into Your hands I commend my soul.*

Linda was grabbed suddenly by the wrist and felt herself being pulled off balance, her ankle swept out from under her as she dropped to the ground, her arm pinned behind her. Rope was securely tied around her hands. "It would have been easier to drug her," said one of the figures, fighting Linda's ineffectual struggles.

"The blood must be pure, untainted by chemicals," replied the other.

Linda was terrified not knowing the meaning of what she was hearing but realizing she was not going to live through the night. Pushing away from her captors, she ran for the cell door, her wrists still tethered behind her back.

The hooded figures grabbed her as she screamed in terror. She managed another scream for help before a hand clamped so tightly over her mouth that her teeth cut into her lip, and she kicked desperately as she was lifted off the ground.

"I wish we could just break her neck here and now and be done with it," she heard a voice say.

"No," the other replied. "She must be cleansed before we take her blood, and the blood must be fresh for the ceremony." The thick folds of the scarf were stuffed into Linda's mouth and pulled tight around her head, even as she continued to buck against her captors, trying frantically to free herself, while they carried her down the hall to the preparation chamber.

∽

Thorold parked his car in the O.N.E. lot and took a moment to study the blueprints Willy had given him, marking the elevators, supply storage closets, staircases, as well as his objective. Taking a deep breath, he whispered, "It's showtime."

Matching his pace to the others, Thorold walked slowly, his shoulders hunched, without talking. Each worker seemed lost in their own world, and he was easily able to blend with the others. He walked up to the security desk, where the man on duty looked him over closely, then suddenly reached into a desk drawer. Instinctively Thorold reached for his gun before remembering that his weapon was hidden in his car.

"Put your thumb on the machine," the guard ordered, holding out a fingerprint detector. "You know the drill."

Thorold obeyed, hoping he was touching the unit's sensor in the appropriate way. The guard paused, looked at the screen, then said, "Have a nice night, Mr. Nidd."

Breathing a sigh of relief, Thorold headed for the storage closet nearest the elevator and pulled out some spray cleaner and rags, stuffing them in the pockets of his overalls and hitting the elevator button.

The elevator dropped slowly to his floor and because the building was almost deserted, he was startled when the door opened and Len Parker, holding a cell phone, stepped out.

Thorold quickly took out the cleaner and sprayed the lobby mirror, ignoring Parker as he began polishing the glass. As he moved down the hall, Thorold heard him say, "I'll be back in an hour, and I don't want to be disturbed."

Before the elevator doors could close, Thorold stepped inside and hit an upper floor button. Through the closing door he saw Parker glance back, then shake his head and continue on his way.

Thorold got off in a low-security area of the building where the workers were mostly clerks handling routine communications, and a security guard patrolled the halls. He walked past two men emerging from the rest room, and as Willy had instructed, walked over to a drinking fountain and looked up at the ceiling where, according to the plans, false tiles concealed a crawl space for repairs and mainte-nance. He leaned over to take a drink of water, listening for anyone in the area, then moving quickly, he climbed up on the fountain and moved aside the tiles to pull himself into the crawl space.

Chapter 23

WILLY LOOKED AT HIS WATCH. It was fifteen minutes after midnight, which meant that Thorold was either safely in the building, captured, or dead. Whatever the case, there was nothing else Willy could do. There was nothing anyone could do. Either they would stop the Day of Wonders or life as they had known it would be changed forever. All they could do now was wait.

Suddenly a beeping sounded on the computer terminal. "Willy!" Cindy cried. "The computer has decoded that last line on the CD."

Willy wheeled over to the monitor and stared at the screen. "Yes!" he shouted. "We're in! The last program I used cracked it. We'll finally see what all the fuss was about." He hurried over to the VR equipment and, grabbing the goggles, excitedly put them on.

"What do you see?" asked Cindy tensely.

"Nothing!" replied Willy dejectedly, his shoulders sagging. It was the same infinite whiteness, the same bright nothingness. Then, just as he was removing the goggles, Willy spotted something in the far distance, glistening in the bright light, like sunlight reflected on polished metal. He began walking toward it, his eyes widening with horror as he moved close enough to see what it was. Perhaps ten feet high and made entirely from surgical steel was a guillotine, the infamous French execution machine created for the swift beheading of its victims. This was not some artifact, however; it was brand-new, made with the latest materials.

Fascinated, he walked slowly around the guillotine, studying it from all angles, running his hand along the side of its smooth blade, and touching the razor-sharp edge. To his surprise, his finger began bleeding.

"What the . . . ?" he said, startled by the pain, and raised the goggles from his eyes. The blood was real. The virtual reality blade had actually cut his finger.

"Oh, God . . . ," Willy whispered.

"What is it?" cried Cindy. "What happened?"

"Oh, my God," he repeated. "I can't believe it! This is impossible!" He spun his chair around, brushing past Cindy and rolling rapidly across the room. "Helen," he shouted. "Look at my finger!"

"It's bleeding, Willy," his sister said. "I'll get you a Band-Aid."

"No!," he shouted. "You don't understand. I cut my finger in Virtual Reality. I felt the pain, and I bled. But that's impossible. Anything you do in VR can't carry over into reality."

"Willy, relax," said Cindy, coming up behind him. "You probably cut it on something else."

Willy had wrapped a handkerchief around his finger

and was holding it tight. "It was the guillotine," he whispered hoarsely. "It cut me and I'm bleeding real blood."

ঔঽ

The altar was set in a clearing in the woods, their customary gathering place for the ritual preparation on Friday night at midnight when the thirteen would assemble, drawing the sacred circle and secret signs, celebrating the mass with the upside-down cross and the words spoken backward, "Hail, Natas!" punctuating the night air.

Now their faith was being rewarded and they were to be part of the most sacred ritual of all, the ceremony evoking the holy one, the culmination of all they had worked for, all they had believed.

It was a time of exultation as they prepared the sacrifice in the manner required, the doctor attesting to her purity before her cleansed body would be offered up. Her blood had been drained to fill the ornamental pitcher, a golden chalice cup was unwrapped from its velvet shroud, and candles had been set in the prescribed manner on the raised platform, each lit in praise of Franco Macalousso.

Len Parker, distinguished by the most elaborate robe of the thirteen, kneeled in prayer before the altar. His garment was purple and scarlet with gold trim, precious gems sewn into the fabric in symbolic patterns from the time of Sanhein and the ancient worship of the dead. Rising, he pushed back the hood from his head and raised the ornamental pitcher, pouring the steaming blood into the golden cup. Then he lifted the cup to his lips and drained it before holding it out in front of him and turning it smoothly in an arc of 180 degrees. It was pointed in turn to each of twelve hooded figures along each side of a stone walkway, each holding lit torches to illuminate the scene, "Speak to the world as you spoke to Eve," Parker intoned.

"Let the Day of Wonders begin!" said the twelve in unison.

"When she plucked the apple from the tree," continued Parker.

"Let the Day of Wonders begin," they chorused.

"Let each man see his heart's desire."

"Let the Day of Wonders begin."

"And believe that our path will take him higher."

"Let the Day of Wonders begin."

"The real wonders are pride and greed."

"Let the Day of Wonders begin."

One of the hooded figures struck a bell, while another moved to a large upside-down cross that had been soaked in kerosene. As the sound of the tolling spread through the clearing, the second hooded figure used his torch to ignite the cross.

"And those shall be our apple tree," Parker continued.

"Let the Day of Wonders begin."

ဝါ

George Hilliard opened one eye as he heard his anxious dog whimpering, whining, and turning in tight circles.

"I just walked you at eleven," said George groggily. "It's only been a couple of hours. Go back to sleep, Max."

The animal continued whining, then barked sharply.

Frustrated, George rose, putting on his clothes, and stumbled around until he found his glasses.

"A man needs a good night's sleep, Max," he said.

The dog wagged its tail, anxious to get going, and the two walked out to the street. The houses around them were dark and silent; cars cruised the streets and no one else was out for a late night stroll.

"Are you finished yet, Max?" asked the man, and in response, the dog tugged on the leash, anxious to go farther. Together, they entered a nearby park where Max usually could find a squirrel or rabbit to chase. But none of his prey were out and about, at least not that George could see. "Even the rabbits have to sleep sometime, Max," he said. "Now can we go back home?"

The dog looked up at the man, reluctantly turning to leave, then stopped abruptly, a low growl rising from its throat. Whining, he pulled the man toward a clump of bushes. It was there, amid piles of leaves and other debris that the naked body of a young woman was dumped, carelessly tossed aside.

Reluctantly, George nudged the body with his foot, but there was no response. He kneeled down, trying to see in the dim moonlight through the leafy covering of the trees overhead. It was then that he saw her wrists tied behind her back, her feet bound at the ankles, her mouth gagged, and her throat slashed from ear to ear.

Standing abruptly, he gasped for air, his stomach queasy as he pulled his dog back from the corpse. Turning, vomiting over and over again, his stomach heaved until he felt light-headed and barely able to breathe.

"Help . . . ," whispered George, pulling Max back onto the path. "Got to find . . . help . . ."

∾

"Welcome to the Day of Wonders" read the words on the computer screen that was being watched intently by Willy and Helen. "For God doth know that on this day your eyes shall be opened, and ye shall be as gods."

"Do you realize what this means, Helen?" Willy was saying. "Everything that happens inside that world is for real! When humanity faces that guillotine tomorrow, they're really going to die."

"Unless Thorold can get that virus uploaded first," Helen replied hopefully.

Listening nearby, Cindy felt the surface of Willy's work-table and found the goggles, stroking them with her hand. Overwhelmed by curiosity she put on the goggles but there was only darkness. Then she heard a voice saying, "Welcome to the Day of Wonders" and saw a sudden bright flash. In the VR world that had engulfed her, she realized she was seeing for the first time.

"I can see . . . something," she whispered in amazement as she stared into the all-white world, seeing the opposite of darkness for the first time. It was then that she sensed the presence before she saw the approaching figure. Franco Macalousso, wearing a flowing white robe bleached to a dazzling purity, walked up to her, smiled, and said, "Hello,

Cindy." His voice was that of the Messiah. And she stared openmouthed and thrilled by the first image she had ever seen.

"I'm glad you could be the first," Macalousso said, his voice gentle and soothing, like a thick blanket on a bitterly cold night.

"Y . . . You're the Messiah," she stammered.

"Yes, I am, so don't look so frightened," Macalousso replied. "There's nothing to be afraid of. On the contrary, you're about to experience the power of the Day of Wonders."

"I can see. I can see!" Her voice rose excitedly as she realized what was happening, her face lit with a look of amazed delight.

"That's right, Cindy," Macalousso continued. "You have beautiful blue eyes, perfect for your lovely face. And now there's a whole world waiting for you, a world of bright skies and beautiful sunsets, a world beyond your wildest dreams, beyond the hopes you have carried in your heart of hearts. This is my gift to you, Cindy. You can see this world but you will also see in the real world as well. When you return you will no longer be blind."

Cindy stared, uncertain what to believe. She knew that for Willy, the headset meant he could walk, even if only inside his mind. But she had been blind, truly blind, and there was no way her mind could create the illusion of sight without a memory of what vision was. "My eyes," she whispered. "They're real?"

Macalousso smiled. "On this special day, you and all of my people will achieve what is your innermost longing. The

Day of Wonders has arrived. The time for illusions is over. Everything you see is real. All you have to do is believe, Cindy. Believe in me. Trust in me. I am the one who gives you your most precious desire. Believe and all you have ever hoped for will be yours."

"I do believe, oh blessed one," she said, tears streaming down her face. She wiped away the tears, then looked down at the wetness glistening on her finger. It was the first time she had ever seen a tear. "Oh, dear Messiah, I do believe," she said sobbing. "Tell me what to do and I will do it. I will do anything for you."

Macalousso's voice now changed, becoming lower with a harder edge. "Renounce Jesus, Cindy," he commanded. "Tell Him He has no place in your life now. Let Him know that you have tasted the fruit of knowledge and that you've seen the truth."

"I . . . I don't understand," she whimpered.

"What has Jesus ever done for you?" Macalousso demanded. "You were blind and He let you stumble through the darkness, but I gave you sight. Renounce Jesus, take my mark and pledge your eternal allegiance to me, the one, true god!"

Cindy looked at him for a moment, then smiled and held out her hand. "I do!" she said joyously.

Franco Macalousso covered her hand with his own and she felt a warmth pass between them. Then he released her to reveal a mark on her flesh: the number 666.

Chapter 24

THOROLD STONE ADJUSTED to the crawl space where he studied the maze of pipes and conduits that formed a virtual cardiovascular system for the building. He located the VR lab and the location of the main alarm console, marking them on the blueprint Willy had given him, and began moving along the pipeline as quickly and quietly as he could. Finding the steel box marked Security, he carefully opened it, staring at the microchips and wires of an elaborate circuit board. "They're color-coded, Thorold," Willy had told him. "If you clip them in the proper order, you can disable it."

He shined his flashlight on the circuits, locating the green, blue, black, and white wires, but there was no red one! Willing himself to be calm, he cut the green wire as instructed, eliminated the white wire from consideration by guesswork, then considered the blue and black. Again acting on instinct, he chose the black wire and holding his breath, he cut it.

◌

The cell phone rang in the hideout, the sound exploding in the empty room. Jumping at the noise, Helen realized how tense they had all become.

"Ronny?" asked Helen, answering the phone. "Thank God you got my message. Willy's cracked the code. We can get into the Day of Wonders program. You better get back here right away."

Turning off the phone, she turned to Willy, his hand shaking as he tried to light a cigarette. An ashtray was already filled with the partially smoked butts, he had been chain-smoking for the last hour. "It just doesn't make any sense, Helen," he said to her. "This is more than a device that stores images. Whatever we're dealing with here is not just technology. It's something more."

Helen was startled by his words. "Images?" she repeated. "Is that what you said?"

"That's right," he replied. "We're just dealing with a bunch of images electronically stored on . . ."

"That's it, Willy," Helen interrupted excitedly. "Images."

"That's what? What are you trying to say?"

"The Bible, Willy. Look . . ." Helen found a Bible and rapidly flipped through the pages. "'And he had power to give life unto the image of the beast,'" she read. "'That the image of the beast should both speak, and cause that as many as would not worship the image of the beast should be killed. And he causeth all, both small and great, rich and poor, free and bound, to receive a mark in their right hand, or in their foreheads: and that no man might buy or sell, save he that had the mark, or the name of the beast, or the number of his name.'"

As Helen continued quoting the passage, Goss returned from a short walk outside for some fresh air. He listened, then began speaking from memory as Helen paused. "'Let him that hath understanding count the number of the beast: for it is the number of a man; and his number is Six hundred threescore and six.'"

Helen nodded. "The images. Willy said that the CD was nothing but images, and that's when I realized what we were dealing with."

"Aw, come on, Helen," Willy entreated. "Get a grip on yourself. This is real life, not some horror movie."

"I'm afraid it's about to become one," she replied grimly.

✺

"What a terrible thing to happen on the Day of Wonders," said one of the police officers, standing in the woods, staring down at Linda's corpse.

"Probably another Hater murder," muttered his partner.

"Ritual killing, if you ask me," interjected one of the detectives. "Didn't know that was part of Christianity. More the kind of thing we used to see with Satan worshipers."

"Slap in the face to the Messiah, if you ask me," said the coroner's investigator as he carefully loaded the corpse into a body bag. "A great blessing and some people still act like animals."

✺

Cindy was smiling as Willy entered. Her sunglasses were back in place, her right hand hidden from his view.

"You really are handsome, Willy," she said quietly.

"That's what everyone without eyes tells me," said Willy, rolling over to the computer system.

"No, I'm serious," she said. "I knew you had a beautiful heart. I just didn't know you were so good-looking."

"Please, Cindy, not now," he said. "I've got to try and figure this out. Somehow, they've invented a machine that let's you experience in the real world what happens in virtual reality. They've joined both worlds. I don't know how it works, but unless we can stop it, Parker's plans may well become a reality. He has the power of life and death over the whole world. I just hope Thorold can . . ."

"I have something to tell you, Willy," Cindy interrupted as he rolled over to the computer monitor.

"Can it wait, Cindy?" he asked. "I just want to see where Thorold is. I don't want to radio him unless I'm sure there's no one else around."

"It's important," she said urgently. "Really, really important."

"What?" he asked, annoyed.

"Those white cowboy boots look silly on you," she said with a smile. "No gunslinger in his right mind would wear white boots."

For a moment Willy didn't understand. "Is that all you can talk about?" he asked. "The way I'm dressed? I thought you said it was . . ." He wheeled around and stared at her, his mouth dropping as she lifted the dark glasses, revealing a pair of bright, healthy blue eyes.

ॐ

They had planned for the assault, the only logical move a desperate man could make. Thorold Stone might have come into the building with guns blazing, anxious to avenge a family they were certain he believed was still alive. But Stone was not stupid, which was why they had assigned a team of special agents to anticipate his moves. No one had seen him enter the building, but the portable sensors hidden in the crawl space had tracked him from the moment he made his appearance.

"Everything is working according to plan, sir," reported the agent in charge of the operation. "Stone is doing exactly what we expected him to."

"And is everything in place?" Parker asked, looking up from his desk with a smile.

"Yes, sir," came the reply. "Ready and waiting. The tracking system indicates he's going to drop right into the VR lab."

"Excellent," Parker said.

ॐ

Helen Hannah could not say that her brother's behavior was especially peculiar, not amid all the tension of the situation and the fact that he had been working under such pressure. Maybe he had closed the door behind him because he wanted to concentrate better or to be alone with Cindy. But his dog, Elvis, was becoming restless without him and Helen was becoming concerned. With the dog by her side, she turned the handle to the door and was surprised to find it locked.

"Willy! What's happening . . . ," she called, just as the door opened and Willy, smiling, rolled into the room. As he entered, Elvis emitted a low growl, baring his teeth, then he barked harshly.

"I've been thinking, Sis," said Willy, ignoring the dog. "If Thorold can't get that virus uploaded, then we're going to need to warn everyone. And you're the only one who knows where the other hideouts are."

Helen, unsettled, stared at her brother. There was something different about him, a hardness she had never seen before. "Is the stress getting to you?" she asked with concern.

"I think you should tell me where the other hideouts are," insisted Willy. "In case something happens to you. I'll need to warn the others."

"I can't tell you where the other hideouts are, Willy," she replied. "You know I can't."

"All right, Helen," said Willy, and patted his lap, trying to get Elvis to jump up. Instead the dog backed farther away, growling at his master. "I made a spiritual decision," he announced. "I finally decided that I could not live my life on the edge. I have to commit and I finally saw the truth."

The conversation was suddenly interrupted by John Goss's angry voice. "Nice try, Willy," he said angrily as he entered the room, bringing Cindy with him. To Helen's amazement, Cindy's blue eyes were blazing brightly and she realized the woman was no longer blind.

"Show her your hand, Cindy," commanded John.

Cindy looked defiantly at Goss, then raised her hand so that Helen could see the number 666 on her skin. "She has been marked as Satan's own," said Goss, disgusted.

"Oh, God, no!" cried Helen.

"Yes!" said Willy, rising from his chair. "I told you Macalousso was for real, that he was filled with goodness." He stepped forward, crossing to Helen. Elvis tensed, ready to spring, and she quickly grabbed his collar and held him back.

"The Messiah made us an offer we couldn't refuse," Willy continued as Elvis began barking fiercely. He looked at his sister and shouted, "Tell that damn dog to shut up!" He pulled a gun from his jacket and pointed it at Goss. "Let her go, choirboy!" he said coldly.

Goss released Cindy, who ran to Willy's side, and as he put his arm around her, Helen could see the mark of the number 666 also etched in Willy's flesh.

In shock, tears streaming down her face, Helen could not believe what Willy had done to himself, not just now but for all eternity. By bearing the mark of the Beast, he had made a conscious choice, rebelling against God.

"No . . . No . . . ," stammered Helen. "How could you, Willy? You've seen exactly what's going on, but you fell for it anyway."

"'Fell for it'? You misguided fool!" Willy said, laughing harshly. There was no gentleness left in his voice, no love left for his sister. It was as if he had lost the very essence of what had made him unique, and even the dog that had loved him now saw him as a stranger. "Thanks to Thorold and the CD, Cindy and I got a sneak preview of the power of the Day of Wonders," he explained. "And in less than eight hours, the whole world will know the truth. I just wish I could have seen it sooner."

"It's not the truth!" shouted Helen. "It's a lie, Willy. It's the ultimate lie."

"Save your breath, Helen," John Goss said. "It's no use. His soul is gone. So is his conscience and everything else that was good in him. He's not the Willy you knew. Once they take the mark, there's no turning back."

"That's right, Helen. You listen to old Johnny," Willy mocked. "You're preaching to the perverted."

He and Cindy laughed wickedly and Elvis began barking viciously. "Lie down!" shouted Willy angrily, but the dog ignored the command, baring his fangs instead. "Lie down, I said!" shouted Willy, pointing the gun at the dog and firing a single shot to the animal's head, killing him instantly. Cindy's laughter echoed through the room.

"Now, where were we?" Willy said, turning his attention to Helen once again. "Oh, yes, you were about to tell me where the other Haters' hideouts are."

"No, Willy, I wasn't," replied Helen, remaining outwardly calm, and carefully choosing her words. "I'd rather die."

"Are you sure?" he asked, raising the gun again and aiming it at her chest. "I should have done this a long time ago," he said with a sneer.

"Do what you have to, Willy," she said and started walking toward the door. Without hesitation, Willy aimed the weapon as Cindy's eyes came alive with the anticipation of violent death.

In that moment, John Goss leaped at Willy. "Go, Helen," he shouted as he grabbed Willy's arm, twisting it and moving in front of the weapon. Willy pulled the trigger, cutting down John as Helen ran out the door and down the stairs.

Pushing past the wounded Goss, Willy pursued his sister but slipped and lost his footing, hitting the ground hard. His gun flew from his hand and clattered down the steps where Helen, startled by the sound, looked back. Grabbing the weapon, she continued running.

"Helen!" came a sharp voice in the darkness. "Helen, what's going on?"

"Ronny? Thank God," she cried. "Hurry. We don't have much time."

Willy got up and hurried down the steps as he heard a car's engine roar to life and the squealing of tires fade away. Helen had gotten away . . . for the moment.

Chapter

25

THOROLD PUSHED BACK THE CEILING TILE and looked down into a dark and windowless room. Using his flashlight to check, he saw the floor directly below him was clear of obstacles, and he lowered himself to the floor. Once inside he surveyed the perimeter with the flashlight.

The electronics lab was just as Willy had described it to him, explaining that the mainframe computer was the one he needed. He began studying the equipment, trying to orient himself before he came to a table where a pair of virtual reality goggles lay. At least he was in the right area, he thought.

There was a crackling sound as Willy's voice could suddenly be heard in his earpiece. "Thorold, I hope you can hear me," Willy said over the radio. "I've learned more about the program, and the virus I gave you won't work unless the system is running. The only way to activate it is to put on the goggles. There should be a pair in the lab. Put them on and stay in VR for a couple of minutes. Then you can return and upload the virus. Good luck."

Trusting Willy's judgment, Thorold put the goggles on

and he suddenly heard a voice saying, "Welcome to the Day of Wonders."

☙

The car pulled to a stop in a dark alley a mile from O.N.E. headquarters. "This is it," said Helen, stepping from the car. "Now, beat me up, Ronny."

"What . . . ?" he said in confusion.

"Beat me up," she repeated. "You're about to arrest me and it can't look like I'm going in without a struggle."

"Helen, are you nuts?" Ronny replied. "I can't do it."

"You have to, Ronny," she insisted. "You're a police officer in full O.N.E. uniform. You're trained to take me down. So do it."

"No!" he said, shaken by her suggestion.

"Okay, you coward." She laughed, mussing up her hair, tearing her blouse, and laying on the ground to roll in the dirt. Putting her hands behind her, she said, "Handcuff me."

He reluctantly did as she requested, then helped her back into the car and drove to headquarters.

"Hey, Ron!" shouted the security guard at the entrance. "Helen Hannah! Big-time, baby! You got the one Parker's been after for months. It's bonus time for you!"

Ron laughed. "This little thing? She practically arrested herself," he replied, leading Helen quickly to the elevators.

☙

White. It was all white, just the way Willy had described it before the code was broken. Gradually adapting to the intensity of the light and gaining more confidence, Thorold began to move forward slowly when suddenly, his foot kicked against something. Reaching down, he felt a soft object and picked it up, realizing it was a teddy bear, the same battered brown toy that had been beloved by his daughters. He moved on, listening and watching, then changed direction, clutching the bear to his chest. He heard the faint sound of laughter. Up ahead, on a swing set, laughing happily, were Wendy and his daughters.

"Wendy . . . Maggie . . . Molly . . . ," Thorold shouted, running toward them and waving the teddy bear as tears streamed down his cheeks. "It's me, Daddy. I can't believe . . . It's been so long, so long . . ."

The three looked over to the running figure, smiling, but said not a word. As he came closer, another figure appeared, Franco Macalousso, the Messiah. "Hello, Thorold, my son," he intoned. "Welcome to the Day of Wonders. I've been waiting for you."

"Macalousso . . . ?" Thorold stopped and stared, looking over again at his children. He knew he was in a virtual world, yet it seemed more real than reality itself. "How can this be?" he asked. "What is this place?"

"I guess you might say that it's a little bit like heaven, Thorold," Macalousso replied. "It's the Day of Wonders."

As Thorold stared, his daughters looked at him, and excitedly called out, "Daddy! We miss you, Daddy."

Wendy, her voice pleading, said, "Don't abandon us again. You've got to open your mind this time. Listen to him. It's the only way."

"Look at their faces, son," said Macalousso. "Look at Wendy, at Maggie and Molly. They're exactly as you remember them, because they are inside of you. Everything is inside of you. That's what I'm here to teach the world. That's what the Day of Wonders is all about." He smiled benevolently, then continued. "The Day of Wonders is different for everyone. For you it is being reunited with your family. For others it is another private joy, whatever their heart desires. All you have to do is accept me and who I am. And anything you can imagine will come to pass; anything you believe will be yours, but not just in here and not just with the goggles. It will be real everywhere."

"What if I don't?" asked Thorold. "What if I don't accept you? What then? And what about the Christians? What happens to them now?"

Macalousso smiled like an indulgent parent gently reproving a petulant child. "Thorold, I'm here to offer you anything and everything you want," he said. "Don't you understand? There is no limit to the fulfillment of your desires. These Haters stand in the way of your dreams, just as they stand in the way of my plans for the whole world."

Thorold looked over to his family again. Standing together now, with Wendy smiling and holding Maggie's and Molly's hands. The little girls looked expectant as if waiting for his decision, a decision that would reunite them all.

"You know, I was wrong about you," said Thorold. "I'm embarrassed to say it now, but I actually thought you were an alien."

Macalousso laughed, sharing Thorold's amusement. "I know," he said. "But now that you can see the truth, all you have to do is take my mark of allegiance. It's similar to when you joined the police force, when you became a special agent for One Nation Earth. Only now, you'll have everything you've ever dreamed of. All you have to do is extend your hand and give me your allegiance."

Thorold took one last look at Wendy and the children. He wanted to run to them, to hold them in his arms, to kiss their sweet faces. But he suddenly remembered the seashell on the beach and all he had learned during his hours of talking with Helen. Maggie and Molly were not Maggie and Molly. Wendy was not Wendy. As much as he wanted to believe it, as much as he wanted to run to them, he knew it was wrong, a cruel deception.

"You can offer me anything you like," said Thorold. "But Helen was right. You don't know the first thing about the love of a father for his child, or the love of God for His creation. I cannot give allegiance to someone like you. I choose to believe in a Creator who would die for His creation, not one who would make them die for him. God gives life. God loves life. You love nothing but yourself."

"My son, you've got to . . . ," Macalousso began.

"I'm not your son, Satan!" Thorold shouted. "You are a liar and the father of lies! I can't believe I didn't see it sooner. And whatever those . . . those things are over there . . . they aren't my family. I know where my family really is."

Macalousso's face hardened; his voice grew cold. "You

say you've made your decision. Let's see if you're ready to pay the price."

Thorold smiled and said, "He already has."

As a horrified Thorold watched, Wendy and the children began to scream in agony, their heads twisting into grotesque shapes as their flesh melted away and their bones softened. They were turning into hideous creatures, as ugly as hate, as ugly as greed and lust and gluttony. Screeching, the three demons took to the air, a foul stench left in their wake.

"You've made your decision, Thorold Stone," Maca-lousso thundered. "Now you must pay the price."

∽

Overlord Parker knew the master's plan must have worked; it had to work. The Messiah could not be stopped. Len Parker would have liked to destroy Agent Stone himself, but he knew that was not his privilege. Yet, perhaps if he hurried, he could see the fate the Messiah had in store for the traitorous agent.

Parker rushed to the VR lab and unlocked the door. The lights were ablaze and Thorold was standing by the table, with the goggles on his head. But there was no mark on either of Thorold's hands, and he was struggling to remove the goggles, his wrists trembling as he used all his strength to pull them away from his eyes. This was not what Parker had expected, but there was nothing he could do. The Messiah was in charge. Whatever was happening was taking place in the world only seen through the goggles. Quietly Parker shut and relocked the door, returning to his office.

There were two uniformed O.N.E. guards, each bearing the mark of the beast on his hand. Their faces seemed half human, half demon, as they grabbed Thorold's wrists before he could take off his goggles.

Leaning into the guard on his right, he brought his knee to his chest, and kicked out at the guard on his left. The blow was hard, yet the man did not flinch. Reversing the action, Thorold led left and kicked right, again connecting solidly. Again the guard did not react.

The guard on his left moved behind him, still holding his wrist, then put his hand on Thorold's shoulder, pulling it back and forcing him forward. At the same time, the second demonic creature punched him twice, once in the stomach and once in the jaw.

Thorold dropped to the ground, fighting for air, as blood pooled in the corner of his mouth. He was then hauled to his feet and marched through the mist until a new object came into view, the same guillotine on which Willy had cut his finger. The blade was ready to be dropped and Franco Macalousso stood at the lever, regarding Thorold with disgust.

"Everything in here is real, isn't it?" demanded Thorold. "The whole world is going to be given the choice of worshiping you or dying. What a pathetic creature you are, just smoke and mirrors. You live on human weakness while God gives us strength."

"I don't have to make them worship me, Thorold," Macalousso sneered. "They'll worship me because I can offer them anything they want. Whatever is in your heart of hearts. Do you covet your neighbor's wife? Your lust is fulfilled beyond your wildest dreams. Do you want wealth? I can deliver it. All your petty desires will be granted. Worship me? They'll praise my name from the moment they wake in the morning and I'll be the last word they utter at night. They'll eat up what I offer. And if they don't . . . You're right, Thorold Stone. They'll die. Everything or nothing, and either way, I win."

Thorold was led to the guillotine, the two guards roughly positioning him so he was looking up at the Messiah, his neck exposed to the blade and his arms and legs bound. He was calm, no longer struggling, and seemed to be accepting his fate.

"I've seen who you really are because I've said no," he told Macalousso. "But what about the ones who say yes? When do they find out who you really are?"

"They know." Macalousso laughed. "Do you think I seduce them through hypnosis? They know I'm the Antichrist, but they're so blinded by their petty desires for instant pleasure and gratification, they happily renounce the One who came before. I give them their hearts' desires and they give me their souls."

"And when do they learn what eternity is going to be like for them?" Thorold persisted.

"Tomorrow," said Macalousso. "For twenty-four hours they will indulge in every fantasy they have ever had. There will be no restraints, no one stopping them. But twenty-four hours after taking my mark, they will know the truth. Their souls will be mine. And once you've taken the mark, there's no turning back."

Thorold stared at Macalousso, then up at the blade. Its heavy steel strained against its constraints.

"Lord, I didn't honor You with my life," whispered Thorold. "But by Your grace, may I do so in death."

Macalousso sneered. "Touching!" he said, releasing the switch and sending the blade hurtling downward. The last thing Thorold heard was an explosion, then everything went black.

Chapter

Thorold! Thorold!" It was Helen's voice. "Thorold. Are you all right?"

He opened his eyes to find himself back in the VR lab, with Helen kneeling beside him, holding the goggles she had just removed from his eyes. Ron stood nearby with his gun in hand. The computer to which the goggles had been attached was sparking and sputtering from the bullet holes Ron had shot into it.

"Helen! Thank God!" Thorold cried. "It was real, everything that happened in there, a different dimension."

"I know," she replied, helping Thorold up. She rubbed her finger gently against his lip, then held it up so he could see the blood on it. "Ron and I got here in time to hear your decision, Thorold," she continued. "It was the right one, but I think you know that. I'm just so proud of you!"

"Where's Willy?" asked Thorold. "Now that we know what this is all about, we need him to—"

"He broke the code," she interjected. "He tried on the goggles. Both he and Cindy met Macalousso in there, too."

"My God, Helen. What happened? What was he offered?" Thorold asked.

"His legs," she replied. "I never knew how badly he felt about being in that wheelchair. I thought he had adjusted. I thought . . ."

"He chose his legs?" asked the incredulous Thorold. "He chose his legs over his soul?"

She nodded. "He wears the mark of the Beast, Thorold. I only wish—"

"Don't," Thorold interrupted, taking her by the arms and looking in her eyes. "Don't you dare feel responsible for a decision that Willy made. You have no idea how seductive that world can be, how appealing it is. All you have to do is pledge allegiance to the man who brought peace throughout the world and you can have anything you desire, any pleasure. What you don't know is that such pleasure is yours for only twenty-four hours. Then Satan has you for eternity." He paused and then asked, "What about Cindy?"

"She chose her eyes," Helen answered

"At least Willy's call makes sense to me now," Thorold mused.

"What call?" asked Ron.

"Willy radioed me," Thorold explained. "He told me to put the goggles on. He knew what I'd find. He thought I'd give my soul to Macalousso." He turned to Helen. "There's this guillotine. I don't know if it's there for everyone, but when I told Macalousso that I chose God, he had these . . . these creatures strap me onto it. Macalousso had just released the blade. A second more and I would have been dead no matter what Ronny's bullets did to the computer." He turned to Ronny. "We have to work fast," he said. "With that uniform, do you have full access to all parts of this building?"

"Everything but the executive floor, and that's not a place where they keep the equipment," Ronny answered.

"I'm not worried about the equipment," Thorold replied. "Everything that matters is in this lab. But there's some good people who are locked up in here somewhere. They're going to be the first ones fed into the Day of Wonder Program."

"I'll do my best to find them," Ron promised.

"I know you will," replied Thorold. "I'm just sorry I let things go so long. Sometimes we cling to false hopes. And I thought Cindy was the blind one." He shook off his self-pity. "Get moving," he said. "We don't have much time."

Ron crossed to the door and opened it slowly, then hurried out. So long as he was wearing his uniform, he knew he was safe. He didn't want them to find Helen and Thorold, though.

Meanwhile, Thorold took a look at the equipment Ron had destroyed, following the wiring to a machine in which everything seemed to connect. It had to be the mainframe Willy had told him about. Taking the disc from his pocket, he put it in the drive, found the keyboard, and hit "Enter."

For a few moments nothing happened before a nearby monitor lit up with the words "Uploading Wonder Buster." A bar graph tracked the progress of the program being loaded. "1% loaded." "2% loaded." It seemed incredibly slow.

"We can't both wait to see this happen," he told Helen.

"I have to get out of here. You stay here. Keep the gun and guard this thing with your life. I'll buy you as much time as I can." Grabbing a disk from the lab, he put it in his pocket and hurried out the door as Helen returned to the screen, which now read "3% loaded."

Thorold moved rapidly down the hall, careful to stop at every turn and check to see if anyone was there. Around the corner, suddenly Thorold heard voices coming from the stairwell where an agent named Spencer and Willy Holmes were walking up the steps, checking every floor.

Thorold still had his cell phone Willy had equipped him with, and knowing he was risking his life, Thorold spoke loudly into it, pretending to be in contact with Ron.

"I'm telling you, Ronny, there's no VR lab on this floor. Willy's directions must have been all screwed up. I still have the disc. I've got to find the right floor, use the goggles, and then insert the disc."

Agent Spencer smiled at Thorold's words. He was convinced they were ahead of Stone and that there was no reason to alert Parker.

"There isn't much more time, Ronny," Thorold continued. "If I don't find it and get this disc uploaded—"

"Perfect timing," Spencer whispered to Willy. He started to draw his gun. Thorold, pretending to hear the men for the first time, began running down the hall as if desperate not to be caught with the disc on him.

"Freeze, Stone!" shouted Spencer.

Thorold ignored him, grabbing a trash can and hurling it back toward them. He took a fire extinguisher from the wall, pulled the pin, and released the CO_2 gas, then threw it and kept on running.

"Give it up, Stone!" shouted Spencer. "Every exit is covered. There's no way out."

I don't want to get out, thought Stone. *I just want to keep you away from Helen until the virus has been loaded.*

Two shots were fired and Stone heard the bullets ricochet off the wall. He came to a second stairwell and ran inside, flattening himself against the door. Knowing they would expect him to flee the building, he moved swiftly up the stairs.

Willy and Spencer burst in, then stopped, listening for anything that might give them a clue as to Thorold's location.

"We need to split up," said Agent Spencer. "Take this spare gun and go up the steps. I'll cover the lobby. One of us should be able to find him. There's no other way out."

⚘

"Come on," whispered Helen. "Load faster. You're supposed to be state of the art. Show me what you can do." The screen climbed slowly from "22% loaded" to "23% loaded." *Why did you have to make it so complex, Willy?* she thought to herself.

Meanwhile, Agent Spencer had reached the bottom of the stairwell, gun at the ready. He stepped quietly into the hall, looking in each direction, listening. He assumed Thorold would probably double back upstairs in search of the VR lab, so he moved toward the back stairs. A rustling sound was heard to the left, along with subdued voices. Spencer turned swiftly, gripping his gun in both hands, and assumed a combat stance. Mrs. Davis and a small line of Haters emerged into view, being force-marched by an officer. No one was resisting. No one was out of line. The situation was firmly in control.

"Keep moving," said the officer. Then, turning to Spencer, Ronny asked, "Any trouble, sir?"

"Nothing we can't handle," Spencer replied.

∽

Willy Holmes walked down the hall, holding the gun out in front of him. He was back in the OK Corral, only this time it was all real. This time when he shot, there would be real blood, and a real corpse. He arrived at the last doorway in the hall. If Thorold had come this direction, it was the only place he could be hiding.

Moving slowly and carefully, Willy pushed open the door, leaped inside the room, and swung his weapon from left to right. He was in the employee cafeteria, and he dropped low to see if Thorold was hiding under the tables. Then he moved to the serving line, trying to keep the steam table in front of him in case Thorold was hiding there. Easing his way into the kitchen, Willy aimed his gun above the cabinets and counters, then swept slowly through the room. Still, there was nothing.

Confused, Willy took the radio and called Spencer. "Nothing up here. I could have sworn he went this way, but he must have headed down." He paused, then added,

"I'm going to go to the VR lab to make sure he doesn't find it."

Thorold listened from inside a walk-in cooler, where he had hidden himself behind crates of milk and fruit juice. It was obvious the chase was over. Thorold had to confront Willy, whatever the consequences. If he reached the VR lab he would kill Helen and stop the virus upload.

Thorold waited until Willy was off the radio, then he threw himself against the door, opening it so fast that Willy panicked and fired a shot into the wall. "A guy could freeze to death in there," quipped Thorold.

"Give me the disc, Thorold," said Willy.

"But Willy, don't you see that you're making a terrible mistake?" Thorold replied.

"Just give me the disc."

How long would it take for the virus to be loaded? How long had it been? And how long could he stall?

"Please, Willy, just listen to me. I've got new information. It should fascinate a guy with your interest in electronics. It's really incredible."

Willy aimed his gun at Thorold, then angrily repeated, "The disc!"

Thorold shrugged, then reached inside his pocket.

"Freeze! Hands up!" ordered Willy.

Thorold held up his hands, trying to keep his voice calm, as he said, "The disc is in my pocket."

Willy stepped forward, pressing the gun to Thorold's temple and, slipping his hand in his pocket, removed the disc.

"Your believer friends are going to die, Thorold," he sneered. "All because you couldn't read a map. Too bad you never . . ." Willy stopped, his eyes widening, realizing the disc he was holding was not the one with the virus.

"Where's Helen?" he demanded, and activated his radio to summon Agent Spencer.

∽

Helen felt desperate as she sat on a chair, alternately watching the door to the lab and the computer screen where the virus had reached 92 percent completion.

Below her, on the first floor, Agent Spencer switched his radio to the tactical frequency, alerting his security team to converge on the VR lab. Willy hadn't been sure if Helen was there with the virus disc, but if she was, they had to stop her.

Len Parker had heard the call from Spencer and made his way quickly to the lab, opening the door and seeing Helen waiting nervously. "Helen Hannah," he said, "the most hated woman on the planet."

Helen stood, making certain her body blocked the monitor where the virus had just moved to 93 percent completion. "The most hated woman on the planet?" she repeated. "My ratings at the network were never that good." Her heart was pounding as she fought to remain calm.

"I guess it's safe to say you're not here to worship the Messiah," said Parker.

"I'd rather die," declared Helen.

"What a wonderful coincidence," said Parker, grinning. "That's exactly what I had in mind." He drew his gun, thinking how he would have liked to torture Helen, but that such pleasures would have to be forgone in the interest of time. It was the Day of Wonders, and in a few hours nothing would be the same.

"Sir! Not in here!" said Ronny, bursting in.

Startled, Parker turned, then, seeing the uniformed officer, relaxed.

"You're right," he said. "Take her downstairs. Let her blood mingle with all the others."

Ronny crossed to Helen, noticing the monitor as he did so. Careful to position himself and Helen to block the screen, he began searching her, then slowly took his handcuffs from his uniform belt and locked her wrists behind her.

"What are you waiting for?" asked the annoyed Parker. Who cared if she was hiding a weapon? He could not be hurt. This was the Day of Wonders, and as the Messiah had promised, life could only get better for the faithful. "Take her downstairs," he repeated.

Ronny did not move, hoping he could still stall for time, but with no idea how to do it.

"Is there a problem?" Parker asked angrily.

Before Ronny could speak, Agent Spencer rushed into the lab, gun drawn. Seeing the uniformed officer, he relaxed, lowered his gun, and smiled at Helen.

"Well, Helen Hannah," he said. "It looks like a perfect sweep. Your knight in shining overalls can't ride to your rescue. He was too stupid to find the right room. And now we have you, too . . ."

"Okay, gentlemen," said Parker, "this isn't the time to

gloat. It's the Day of Wonders and we all have work to do. Get her downstairs to the execution chamber. It's about time that we . . ."

Angry voices in the hall interrupted the Overlord as Willy opened the door, escorting the handcuffed Thorold Stone. With him were another agent and Cindy, both brimming with excitement. Cindy felt especially powerful with her new vision and her new friends.

"Him!" shouted Willy, wide-eyed when he recognized Ronny. "He's one of them!" He charged as Ronny moved forward to meet the attack. Even with his upper body, unusually powerful from the years of propelling himself in the wheelchair, Willy was still no match for the better trained Ronny, who held him off.

Parker drew his gun and aimed it at Helen. But just as he began to pull the trigger, Thorold dropped low, like an athlete crouching into a broad jump, his hands still tightly cuffed behind him. Aiming himself at Parker, he leaped at the Overlord, knocking his gun hand askew and sending the bullet flying past Helen's ear to shatter a computer monitor. Parker fell to the ground as Spencer grabbed Thorold, who stomped on the agent's feet, trying to free himself. Spencer barely managed to wrestle him to the ground.

Parker rose to his feet, grabbing Helen around the neck and putting the gun barrel against her temple. "Give it up, turncoat!" he shouted to Ronny. "Give it up or I'll blow her head off right now!"

Ron disengaged from Willy, realizing he had to protect Helen and vie for time. Willy took advantage of the situation to punch Ron in the face, a blow that threw his head back and gashed his lip.

"They're trying to stop the Day of Wonders," shouted Willy as he hurried to the computer. The second agent grabbed Ronny and forced him into a far corner of the room where Helen and Thorold were standing.

Willy checked the monitor and saw that the virus was only at 95 percent. Unless it went to 100 percent, it was useless and knowing how slowly the program loaded, he quickly typed in the code to abort the program. Then, on the screen, the message "96% loaded" appeared.

"Has anyone changed the security clearance?" he asked, frantically typing a different code.

"Why?" said Parker. "What's wrong?"

Willy didn't answer, instead removing the disc from the drive and breaking it. He grabbed the connecting cord and ripped it out before retyping the string of commands to abort the system. "97% loaded," read the next message. Frantic, he took his gun and shot the Central Processing Unit, the heart of the computer. Sparks flew and a flame erupted, then died. The unit was worthless.

"98% loaded" read the screen.

"No!" shouted Willy. "This is impossible. This is impossible."

Len Parker stared in amazement, sweat beading on his forehead. All the preparation, all the work, and the Day of Wonders was about to be undone.

"Impossible!" said Willy, tearing the monitor from the unit.

"With God, all things are possible," said Helen, smiling.

Ignoring her, Willy ripped out all the wires attaching the CPU to the main computer. He threw the equipment across the room, then picked up the obviously disconnected monitor, wires dangling from the back. Yet as he watched in horror, the screen changed to "99% loaded."

"No! No! This can't be. I designed the program myself," he screamed.

"Ever hear of God's unlikely vessel, Willy?" asked Helen quietly.

They all watched as the screen read, " 100% loaded. Fully activated." In shock Willy whispered, "The virus is loaded. The Day of Wonders program has been destroyed."

For Helen, Thorold, and Ronny it no longer mattered what happened to them. Live or die, they had given the world one more chance to return to God.

Parker turned to the three Christians and shouted, "You may have stopped the Day of Wonders, but you can't stop prophecy. I won't let you interfere." He raised his gun to execute them where they stood.

Then, as if they were on a windswept desert instead of inside a sealed electronics lab, a funnel cloud rose between the Christians and Parker, like the dust devils Thorold had seen in the Southwest when he and Wendy had visited Tucson. As he stared in amazement, he heard Helen whisper something about a voice out of the whirlwind.

Enraged, Parker fired his gun through the whistling clouds, but the bullet did not penetrate. It was caught as if in a revolving door, spinning around and returning in Willy's direction. Before he could cry out, he dropped to the ground, a bullet hole through his heart.

Parker tried to move to the side of the whirlwind. But, it became larger, stronger, and even thicker, engulfing him and capturing Spencer and Walker in its vortex as Cindy pressed herself against the far wall, desperate to escape. Raising her hands as if she could ward off its power, she saw the mark on her hand. All else had turned as black as when she was blind, the mark being the last thing she saw as she was sucked into the swirling inferno that had trapped the others.

Helen, Ronny, and Thorold ran to the door and hurried down the hall.

"No! No! Get back here, Christians. You can't escape!" Parker's voice rose in a cry of anguished pain as the three rushed through the corridors, stopping only to allow Ronny to remove Thorold's handcuffs.

The sounds from the lab grew louder as they heard the winds inside grow to the hurricane force of a howling banshee, mixed with cries of terror and pain. Then, almost as quickly as it all began, it was over and there was total silence. The pressure against the door had ended.

Thorold looked at Helen and Ronny. They knew what they had to do and together they returned to the lab door. Helen and Ronny stepped back as Thorold reached for the handle, opening it slowly while the three of them moved inside as one.

"The room is empty," said Ronny.

"There's nothing here," said Helen, in shock. "No computers. No furniture. No people."

"Not quite everything is gone," said Thorold, spotting what he at first thought was a small scrap of paper in the corner. He walked over to pick it up, and saw that it was the photograph of Wendy, Maggie, and Molly he had been carrying with him. On one side were their happy faces. On the other were the words "The truth has set us free."

Epilogue

THE ONE NATION EARTH prison transport van, fully loaded with Haters, was parked in a darkened lot behind the headquarters building. There were no guards in the vehicle and one of the former prisoners sat in the driver's seat with the motor running.

Helen, Ronny, and Thorold ran out of the building and jumped into the van. "Move it!" shouted Ronny as the door closed and the driver accelerated onto the street.

Thorold, breathless yet exhilarated, turned to Anna Davis and asked, "Remember me?"

"I'm glad the Lord has opened your eyes, son," she said with a smile.

"I'm so sorry for all that you've been through," Thorold replied. "I didn't know. I thought you were . . . well, I was deceived."

Holding on to the seat backs to keep her balance, Anna Davis stood and walked over to Thorold and gave him a hug. "You're forgiven," she said. "We all are." She stepped back, looking him in the eye, then took his hand and held it tenderly.

"All our losses become tolerable if the end result is another soul saved," she told him. "That's worth more than the whole world."

Smiling, she looked past Thorold as if seeing something the others could not, but the joy on her face was contagious. As though led by some divine choirmaster, Mrs. Davis began singing "Amazing Grace," and the others joined in.

As the van moved into the night, Thorold, with tears streaming down his face, joined the rest, singing, "that saved a wretch like me."